DISNEY

SNOWWHITE

FAIR &
SINISTER
HEART

Published by Disney Press, an imprint of Buena Vista Books, Inc.
No part of this book may be reproduced or transmitted in any
form or by any means, electronic or mechanical, including
photocopying, recording, or by any information storage and
retrieval system, without written permission from the
publisher. For information address Disney Press,
1200 Grand Central Avenue, Glendale, California 91201.

Printed in the United States of America

First Hardcover Edition, March 2025
1 3 5 7 9 10 8 6 4 2
FAC-004510-25009
Library of Congress Control Number: 2023940577
ISBN 978-1-368-09771-0

Design by Gegham Vardanyan

Visit disneybooks.com

SUSTAINABLE FORESTRY INITIATIVE

Certified Sourcing

www.forests.org
SFI-01681

Logo Applies to Text Stock Only

Disney

SnowWhite

Fair &
Sinister
Heart

By Lauren Blackwood

Disney PRESS

LOS ANGELES · NEW YORK

Once upon a time, there was a girl with
big dreams who fell into a deep sleep...
and opened her eyes to a nightmare.

S he winced, her eyelids fluttering against the sun glaring through her dark lashes before she could finally
open them, slowly. Light cut sharply across her vision,
soft-colored rays shimmering and refracting as if off a
prism. She blinked a few times, squinting to adjust to the
brightness as she sat up.

Her head reeled—she had sat up too quickly—she
pressed her palm against her forehead to ease it, slowed her
movements. Her limbs felt as if they were moving through
sludge. It was that strange sickness one felt after either

not napping long enough or napping far too long, and yet she did not remember ever going to sleep. But she had to be dreaming. She *must* be, because the woods around her didn't look quite right.

The trees were all shaped like real trees, at least for the most part—large red-brown trunks, branches that reached in all directions toward the sky, and green leaves to shade her from the sun. But that was where the similarities ended. The trunks, red-brown as they were, weren't textured like bark, nor did they have the rough matte finish of wood. They had a silkier finish, like a piece of pottery fired, painted, and glossed. Like a swirling of oil paints of gold and brown, buffed to a gorgeous luster. Was it . . . a gemstone? Any remaining doubt vanished when she saw what she had first mistaken for leaves: they were green and hard and bright, but slightly transparent. They looked just like . . . emeralds? That was where the dapples of color had come from. She looked at her skin as the soft light danced on her like fine stained glass.

Beautiful. As if nature itself was cut from royal gemstones. Yet there was something vicious in this beauty . . . an unnatural, inherent wrongness.

And the trees weren't the only things exhibiting this unnatural beauty. She found herself staring in awe at the wildflowers at her feet, their petals made from clear, bright gems. She crouched down and reached out slowly, carefully. But she drew back her hand when a sharp pain ran through her finger, the cushion of it throbbing. She looked at it, frowning slightly, as a small bead of red bloomed. And then she quickly put her finger in her mouth, pressing the wound to her tongue.

Dreams weren't supposed to hurt.

No. This was most certainly not a dream. Besides, she had not even been sleeping before she had opened her eyes; she had been—

She gasped, memories flooding back to her. She was Snow White, crown princess and now runaway, to avoid the murderous attempts of her stepmother, the Queen. The first was in the apple grove with the Huntsman, whose soft heart or guilt had forced him to let her go. Then the encounter with the soldiers: she blushed thinking about brave, handsome Jonathan and his band of thieves, who had saved her life from their attack. She also couldn't forget her seven friends, who had taken her in, protected her.

Then there was . . .

The apple.

Such an ordinary thing to cause so much confusion,

but it was the last thing she remembered before she awoke remembering nothing at all. The apple must have been poisoned in some way. Cursed? Enchanted. How else would she still be alive but not, well . . . *was* she alive?

Wherever Snow White was, she needed to find out, and soon. The people she cared about—her kingdom, her friends—were in trouble.

She sighed and looked around. She had been in the wilderness when she had bitten the apple, too, but at least her friends had been nearby. Here there were no signs of civilization.

It's time to choose your fate, Snow White thought. North, south, east, west. There was no telling which way would lead her somewhere she could find help. So she simply picked a direction and began walking, careful to avoid the sharp flowers scattered all over the ground. She had to find a path soon, as the emerald grass was not much safer for her feet should her shoes wear out.

As she walked, she saw something stalking her within the trees along the side. Something on all fours. But when she blinked, there was nothing but branches and leaves.

This place is playing tricks on my mind, she thought. Every shadow and flicker of light reflected by the gemstones made her more uneasy.

She walked until she came across a wide path. Where there were paths, there were people . . . or big animals. She was on the right track toward *something*. If only there was a river she could follow; towns were usually built close to rivers.

But as it stood, she didn't have any other options.

With nothing but hope in her heart, Snow White again picked a direction and continued on. The sun was behind her, and she tried not to dwell on the fact that it had dropped lower than it was when she had woken up. In a few hours' time it would be evening, and it was probably best if she could find someone who could help her by then.

She tripped as movement caught her eye again. She could see now that what she thought had been stalking her earlier was a furry animal on all fours; she couldn't quite make out what it was, but she still breathed a sigh of relief.

"Oh, hello," Snow White said. Hope filled her gut. She wondered how long the animal had been there, following her. Though that didn't matter as much as that it was *there*, right when she most desperately needed it to be.

"Can you help me?" she asked.

The creature emerged from the shadows of the trees, wolflike in appearance. As it moved closer, Snow White's heart began to pound. It was clear this wasn't any ordinary wolf, no more ordinary than the flowers and trees were.

It was alive, to be sure, but at the same time, how could it have been? What she had mistaken for fur at a distance was actually sharp grayish jewels, catching the late-afternoon sun. Snow White's stomach turned with dread, because the uneven surfaces of its transparent body gave her a warped view of the visceral inner workings of the beast. She distinctly saw the rhythmic pumping of the creature's wet, veiny heart. The thin strands, like little rivers on a map, carrying deep-red liquid through its entire body. The pale crumpled bags of flesh in its chest expanding taut with each breath.

Like a mortal machine. It was a nightmarish thing to behold.

So it took Snow White a moment to swallow a bit of bile and suppress her fear. It was still a wolf, after all, just like those back home. She had talked to plenty of wolves before . . . even if she had not been watching their organs function while she did it.

But she could not very well judge the one creature who might be her only ally in this strange world.

She jolted as the wolf began to growl at her, the vibration more than just guttural. It was like the rumbling of hundreds of small stones. Like an impending rampage.

Her momentary fear had clearly made it nervous.

"It's all right, my friend," Snow White said, reaching her hand out to the creature. "It's just that I've never seen a wolf that—"

But as it snapped its jaws at her, she fell, cringing as she crushed the hard grass beneath her back.

Wherever she was, it certainly wasn't right. At home the animals had always been her friends and most helpful, even the ones she had not met before. She had never heard an animal growl at her in her life.

She dragged herself backward, away from the creature, which watched her but didn't follow. For a moment, it only looked at the area on the ground where Snow White had fallen and the solid grass had been crushed to small chunks and dust. It lifted a paw as if it intended to approach her, then changed its mind and simply growled.

The creature locked eyes with her. The eyeballs, held inside by bundles of veins, shifted over her in quick, eerie movements. There was a lethal coldness in its gaze. Not as an animal would have if territorial or hunting, but as if it felt no desire to protect or eat. It was growling, yet it felt nothing. Snow White suddenly realized it wasn't only the exterior that separated the animals in her world from this one.

Only she realized it too late, because without warning, the creature leapt at her, and Snow White barely had time to shield herself with her arms before—

The hard sound of metal hitting rock erupted around her. A young man had blocked her body from the creature, with his sword pressing against the creature's solid head. He fought it off with a heavy shove.

"Stop!" Snow White cried as he swung. "Don't hurt it!" she yelled as he swung again. He ignored her pleas, backing the creature away from her and into the trees with each strike, until finally it whimpered and retreated into the depths of the woods.

"You could have scared the poor creature off without harming it," Snow White said, glaring at the young man as he stood with his back still facing her and panted from his efforts.

He didn't answer. Instead, he took a step forward, looking out for the creature, as if making sure it wouldn't return. He had meant to save her from an obviously dangerous situation; that much was clear, even if she disliked his methods. Still, part of her was ready to run if she had to. First the flower, then the wolf, now . . .

But when the young man turned to her, he wasn't made of gems and sharp angles. His skin was deep brown, and she could tell his hair, though cropped close to his scalp, would grow in coils if it wasn't cut. He wore heavy boots and fingerless gloves, and his leather tunic was worn but sturdy. He was a person, flesh and blood, like her.

But still, if everything else—plants and animals included—was out to kill her, how could she be sure she could trust this young man?

Yet as he approached her, she felt a wave of relief wash over her, if only it meant she wasn't alone in this strange place.

But when the young man finally gave her a good once-over, he sighed, heavy and defeated.

"Oh, wonderful," he said, though his tone implied the opposite of his words. "Another princess."

S now White stared at the young man for a moment, trying to gauge whether their interaction was truly happening. After all she had witnessed, a regular person seemed strangely out of place.

Also . . . *what* had he just said to her?

"E-excuse me?" she said.

"You look like a noble's daughter," he replied, and it sounded more like an accusation than a comment. "Have you ever worked a day in your life?"

Despite his words, he held out his hand to her, as if he was some sort of gentleman attempting to help her to her feet. Gentleman indeed! *He* wasn't a noble's son—that was for certain. In fact, Snow White had met thieves who behaved better. She refused his help on principle, pushing herself to her feet, despite the aching in her back from falling.

"I've done my fair share of work, thank you very much," she said firmly. After all, once her mother had passed and her father had gone away, the Queen had turned her into nothing more than a servant of the house . . . though perhaps the actual servants were treated better than she had been.

"All I mean is it requires a lot of physical labor to live here," he said, "and there are no special exceptions for princesses. You'll be doing the heavy lifting along with the rest of us." Yet again he said the word *princess* as if he didn't respect the position, at least in terms of this place. His sword flashed, sparkling in the late sun, as he sheathed it. It wasn't an average metal sword, but looked to be carved from solid diamond. "But of course, you're a stardrop, so you wouldn't know. We will have you adjusted soon enough." He looked her over again with a skeptical expression on his face. "Hopefully."

"A stardrop?"

"As in the stars dropped you off." The young man looked around carefully. "Let's walk as we talk, shall we?" And he started off without waiting for her.

Snow White hesitated, weighing her options—stay there and potentially meet up with another wolf and possibly be eaten or follow this rather irritable young man and be led to who knew where. The decision didn't take long, although she wished she had more appealing options. It was better to take her chances with him than with another one of those creatures. And with that, she rushed to catch up.

"What do you mean the stars dropped me off?" she asked. His legs were longer, and it took double the effort to keep up. "I ended up here by biting an apple. . . ." Saying it out loud, she realized it sounded too silly to be true. But then again, she was currently in a world completely made of gemstones, so anything seemed possible. "I think."

"Everyone crashes down here as a shooting star. It's how I knew where to find you." He finally looked at her again, with little if any sign of good humor, despite his tone not being entirely unfriendly, and she suddenly realized that perhaps his slightly murderous expression was only his resting face. "I'm Henry, by the way."

"Snow White."

Henry paused. "All right, *don't* tell me your real name, then."

"That *is* my real name."

He raised a brow skeptically. "Well, I suppose it isn't the strangest name I've heard here."

Snow White tugged her skirt away from some particularly spiny flowers. "And where is 'here' exactly?"

Henry laughed, a bit bitterly, and shook his head. "You bit an apple, you say? For me it was a Turkish delight. The Queen enchanted us."

"The Queen?" And suddenly, the gemstones made sense. The Queen was obsessed with them. Their beauty, their perfection. Creating them was part of the wicked magic she wielded.

Or perhaps the magic wasn't as wicked as the one who possessed it.

But that confirmed it for her: the Queen had indeed tried yet again to be rid of her. Only it wouldn't be for long if Snow White had anything to say about it.

"It doesn't take much, either," he said, shaking his head again. "The smallest offense and, if she feels like it, she'll send your subconscious here. To Diamant."

"Subconscious?" Snow White smoothed her dress, feeling the soft fibers, the threaded seams. Then she looked at the prick on her finger, which was no longer bleeding but still stung a little and was pink all around. "But everything feels so real."

"Our bodies are still asleep somewhere in the real world. I only know that because my sister, Tabitha, took care of my sleeping body before she . . . *offended* the Queen." He hesitated before adding, "You'll meet her, too."

They continued on, with Snow White stepping carefully so as not to trip over any protruding gems. The Queen's idea of beauty certainly was vicious.

"So, what did you do to the Queen to end up here?" asked Henry, without much curiosity. It must have been a question he asked everyone he rescued. "Or what *didn't* you do?"

Snow White sighed, thinking back to the horribleness the Queen had sent the Huntsman—and later her own soldiers—to do. "Nothing. I just . . . exist."

"That sounds about right," he said with a bitter smirk.

"What about you, Henry? What brought you here?"

"My father rejected the Queen's advances." He looked a little uncomfortable. "She didn't seem to care about my father at all . . . but she thinks she can have anything she wants."

At the mention of his father, Snow White thought about her own—about what she had learned about him just before she had bit into the apple. About how all her hopes of finding him, of them taking back their kingdom together, of her ever seeing him again had been dashed. About what the Queen had done to him. "How awful."

"I was his only son, so I suppose she thought that was even revenge for being slighted."

"She's worse than I thought."

Don't be dishonest, Snow White thought, chiding herself. *You know how awful she is.*

"That's not even the worst of it," he said. "When we get to town, ask my sister how she ended up here."

Snow White cringed. After his story, part of her didn't want to know.

"Ouch!" Snow White moved away from the edge of the path, rubbing her calf and frowning at the blade that had scratched her. When she looked up at Henry, he seemed more than a little irritated, rolling his eyes as he looked away from her to study the horizon. Surely he couldn't blame her for not understanding this world after only just arriving. "This emerald grass must cause a lot of trouble."

"The grass is actually jade," he said. Henry walked on, not bothering to wait for Snow White. She caught up. "The leaves on the trees are emeralds. The trunks are tigereye, and the flowers range from diamonds to amethyst to rose quartz. The wolves are . . . well, the wolves are something else." He shrugged, smiling the slightest bit as she gaped at him. "I've worked a lot with precious stones."

"Amazing."

"I mean, it was required knowledge for my profession."

"Were you a miner?" Snow White asked excitedly, thinking of her friends back home.

He side-eyed her. "No."

"What did you do?"

He paused, and suddenly, the light that had graced his eyes extinguished. "Doesn't matter now," he said, and pressed forward.

Henry didn't speak much after that. They continued their hike on the mostly level path, only pausing once, when a flock of cranes made of lapis flew far too close to their heads, forcing them to duck. But Snow White relished that one pause, not because she was tired, but because the blue birds were so beautiful. There were moments to treasure in that strange land, even if none of it should have existed.

The water is as it should be, at least, she thought as Henry led her over a bridge made of black stone. It was good to know that she could at least drink something, even if the plants and animals were inedible.

They walked on for what seemed like miles while the

sun dropped lower and lower, worrying Snow White more than the creatures. She couldn't begin to know what they would use to build a fire or shelter if night fell and they had to spend it in the stone-cold wilderness.

Snow White thought she had known what it was like to be on her feet all day, and she had spent the past few days in the real world in the woods, dodging the Queen's attempts to kill her with the help of her friends. But this was grueling, to the point that she could swear her feet were blistered and bleeding. And when she reached that point, they walked still *more*. She was thankful that by then she had disassociated from her feet completely and they seemed to be moving just fine on their own without her feeling a thing.

But despite all her concerns, she could not help noticing how lovely the sunset was. It was beautiful at home, too, but here every single gem caught the light, reflecting it and rejoicing like a chorus. They had looked lovely earlier, but now they twinkled in all shades and hues, like a canvas speckled by a painter with the flick of a brush. Like rainbow starlight. It looked like magic, even if it was only light.

Finally, Henry gestured in front of them and said, "We're here."

Up ahead, just beyond the trees, was a high black wall

that looked to be made of something like granite, and Snow White was grateful for the sight of it. The sun was dipping below it now, the slight chill of evening was setting in, and she was exhausted. And even though she couldn't see what was inside yet, she knew it had to be safer than what was out here.

At least, she thought so until she saw, held up by two poles, a giant sign that read in large red lettering, *Welcome to Diamant: where her dream is your nightmare.*

Snow White looked at Henry, and he rolled his eyes.

"The longer you're here," he said, frowning, "the more you'll find that some people have a cavalier spirit when it comes to their subconscious being eternally trapped in a strange world." He opened a large gate carved directly into the towering wall. It appeared to be the only way in or out. "If I were you, I would avoid those people at all costs."

S now White could hardly believe what she was seeing. The wildlife made of gemstones had been more than enough fantasy to wrap her mind around, but this? She looked at the fifty or so houses arranged around an open square full of people. At the center was a large well made of shimmery black stone. It sat on three stacked platforms that formed a set of three stairs encircling it. The apparatus that held the bucket consisted of two thick poles that met over the well to form a triangle. It had the look of a monument, more than just a well, so it was fitting that it sat at the very center of the town square.

The place was remarkable. Everything had been

carved from gemstones—but these irregular cuts clearly had been made by human hands rather than magic. And that feat made it even more incredible than the vicious woods around them. And inspiring, in a way. Knowing how resourceful these people were made her hopeful that finding a way home wouldn't be as difficult as she thought.

And seeing so many people there—people just like her—walking around, socializing . . . As happy as they looked, it tightened her throat with emotion. All those people had been enchanted by the Queen—the queen who was now holding her kingdom hostage, ruling them without kindness or mercy. Snow White felt a wave of sadness for the plight of the people trapped there . . . sadness that quickly turned to determination.

She needed to get back home and fix this—quickly. The question was, how?

"Henry's back with the stardrop!" someone called, and Snow White startled as the people in the square started surrounding them with cheerful smiles.

What a relief to find that the people there were friendly. Traveling with Henry for so many hours had started to make her wonder what sort of temperaments she'd be dealing with from the rest of the town.

"Who are you?" someone asked.

"What did you do to get here?" asked another.

"She's pretty. That must be it. The Queen hates not being the prettiest in the room."

"Welcome to Diamant!"

"Wow, that's some yellow dress!"

"What's your name?"

The volley of questions had Snow White snapping her head in every direction. She wasn't sure where to start. Not to mention she had plenty of questions of her own. If she wanted to discover a way home, she needed to find out more about the place called Diamant.

"Can they breathe first?" A young woman, perhaps a little older than Snow White, pushed through the crowd, a pickaxe in her hand. Snow White thought of her seven friends and instantly smiled. "Give them some space, will you?" the young woman said with an air of authority. "I mean, honestly." She stopped in front of Henry and met his gaze. "You're all right."

Henry kissed her head—such a tender gesture from someone who had been so stoic with Snow White not even minutes before. "Of course I am, Tab."

Snow White was struck by how alike they looked—both tall and elegant, with the same beautiful deep brown skin and jeweled brown eyes. She couldn't see much of the woman's hair, as it was wrapped in a sapphire scarf, but a few stray curls stuck out. They couldn't have denied being related if they had wanted to.

Tabitha suddenly flicked Henry in the forehead. Snow White quickly covered her mouth with her hand, pressing back a surprised laugh.

"Ow!" growled Henry, rubbing at the spot and scowling.

"Next time," Tabitha said, planting her hands on her hips with a stern look, "tell me where you're going before you just run off."

"I told you I was fetching a stardrop. You must need to clean your ears."

"No, you said, 'I'll be right back,' and then proceeded to disappear for over four hours."

"Same difference."

Tabitha glared at Henry before shaking her head and grinning. "I'll deal with you later."

She turned to Snow White and sized her up for the first time. She had intense eyes, just as her brother did. Yet her intensity differed from Henry's. His eyes were guarded and irritated. Hers were confidently absorbing what was in front of her as she assessed the situation, yet there was an undeniable patience in them that told Snow White the woman meant her no harm. A small smile graced her lips.

"You're coming with me." She grabbed Snow White's hand and led her out of the throng. Everyone continued to stare as they went by, just as fascinated by Snow White as she was by Diamant.

When they were clear of the town square, Tabitha let go of Snow White's hand. "It's been a while since the last stardrop," she said. "We don't get much excitement around here. Can you tell?"

"Everyone is very friendly," Snow White said.

"We're all a big family, but that doesn't mean they should crowd. Unfortunately, some of them have been here so long they've forgotten their manners."

The two of them wove through the maze of stone houses, which had only small alleys between them. It was a bit like a network, connecting everyone; this seemed like a place where no one was ever left out of daily life. The houses were all individual in form, as if carved by a community of hands. Snow White liked the imperfection of them; it was proof that the Queen had had nothing to do with their construction. These were not magical creations to be used against the people held hostage here. No, this was rebellion—a sign that the people had taken their fate into their own hands, whether the Queen liked it or not. And that gave Snow White more hope than ever.

All the people in Diamant seemed to get along wonderfully. It reminded Snow White of her childhood, of the tight-knit community that was her kingdom, her people. It was a beautiful thought, to have so many people to rely on, even if she could not linger there for much longer. It made her think of her friends back home, who were counting on her. Her seven friends, who had so graciously let her stay in their house. The thieves, who had risked their lives to save her from the Queen's soldiers. And Jonathan, leader of the thieves . . . Her heart danced at just the thought of him.

"I'm sorry, I never asked your name," Tabitha said, drawing Snow White's attention back to her.

"It's Snow White," she said, bracing for the usual reaction.

Tabitha looked surprised, but pleasantly so. "How very original."

"Henry said something similar," Snow White remarked. She didn't mention that Tabitha was a fair bit more polite than he had been about it.

As if reading Snow White's mind, Tabitha said, "I hope he was nice to you. Diamant has turned him into a bit of a beast."

"He had his moments," said Snow White, and Tabitha frowned disapprovingly. "But his intentions were good."

"Loyal and gallant through and through, that boy," Tabitha said, "but with the social skills of a rock sometimes."

Perhaps so. But Snow White felt cozy inside remembering how warmly Henry had greeted his sister. She had sweet people like that waiting for her at home, too.

They entered a small house, and the interior took Snow White's breath away. The outside had been rough stone like the rest, but the inside was sparkling and the vibrant color of violets; it probably would have been translucent if the rocky exterior had not been there. All the walls and countertops looked as if they had been carved from one large stone, smoothed out and connected, shimmering like a starry sky.

"Isn't it exquisite?" Tabitha said proudly. "Most of the houses are carved from granite, like the wall surrounding the town, but Henry carved mine from a geode. I love amethyst, don't you?"

"It's gorgeous," gasped Snow White, running her hand over a smoothed table.

"It may be one of the smaller houses, but it's the prettiest. Please, have a seat, make yourself at home." Tabitha hung her pickaxe from a hook on the wall. "I'll make you a footbath of rock salt. Your feet must be killing you."

"They are, a bit, now that the adrenaline of that walk has worn off," said Snow White, still looking around the house in awe, before sinking into a smoothly carved seat.

"I always try to keep some coals hot when I know Henry's been away, just in case he needs them. And he *always* needs them." Tabitha threw some salt into a stone bowl and put it on the floor as Snow White removed her shoes. She took the kettle from over the coals and poured steaming water in. "It's not boiling, but give it a moment so you don't burn your skin off."

"Thank you so much for this, Tabitha. For everything."

"Oh, it's no trouble at all. I'm so glad you're here."

Snow White wasn't sure how to respond. She didn't say that she *wasn't* glad to be there. Because she *was* there, and until she found a way home, she would remain there. So Snow White supposed, under the circumstances, it was much better to make friends.

In Snow White's opinion, it was *always* much better to make friends.

Snow White eased her feet into the bowl. The water was perhaps still too hot, but it felt good against the slight chill of the evening coming down on them. And her feet *needed* it. Already the heat was distracting her from the aching, and soon the salt would take care of it. It was the nicest thing she had experienced in a while.

"You're welcome to take a bath, as well," said Tabitha, washing her hands in a small basin. "I can show you where it is after your feet are finished."

"No, thank you. I'm fine," said Snow White. "But I would love a glass of water, please."

Tabitha chuckled. "Oh, yes, I forgot. Your mind isn't adjusted to our world yet."

Snow White watched her hostess flick excess water from her fingers into the basin. "Is the water not good for drinking?"

"What you're feeling is exhaustion, Snow White, not thirst." Tabitha dried her hands on her skirt. "Your mind is used to thinking about the needs of your body, but here in Diamant we are not concerned with such things."

Snow White saw some movement from the corner of her eye, and the memory of the wolf made her jerk her head toward it to look. Her heart pounded from the thought of seeing another creature, but all she saw was a bit of dark hair quickly disappear behind a wall. *How very . . .* "Odd."

"It will feel odd until you get used to it. Your physical

body needed food and drink, but all your subconscious needs is some good sleep."

Snow White wiggled her toes, the movement far less uncomfortable than it had been. The salt was working. "But we still feel pain?" she asked, curious.

"Cruel, isn't it?" Tabitha smirked. "The dangers are very real here. If you die in Diamant, well . . . you'll never wake up in the real world."

Snow White cringed. That was a detail she'd never thought to ask about, but it was rather horrifying to consider. *So don't consider it*, she thought, determined. *Just find a way home.*

Snow White saw the movement again, and when she quickly looked, she noticed two blinking brown eyes peering from around the corner. They belonged to a little girl. Snow White smiled, but the girl rushed away.

"That's Mouse," said Tabitha. She opened a large stone barrel and began scooping coal from it into a bucket. "She's a little shy with strangers, but she'll warm up to you soon enough."

Snow White felt her heart droop the smallest bit. "Children so young end up in Diamant? How awful."

"Fortunately, she's the only one."

"Whose child is she?"

"No one's here. It's rare people who are related end up in Diamant. Henry and I are one of the few exceptions." She peered at the spot where the girl had been peeking and lowered her voice. "She was the first-ever inhabitant of Diamant. She's been stranded here longer than anyone. Decades. She doesn't ever talk about it, and who could blame her?"

Snow White could not even imagine being stuck there a week, let alone decades. She thought of the things one would miss in real life while the years went by. Weddings and funerals. Families and friends. They would all keep moving along while the unfortunate person slept their life away.

While *Snow White* slept her life away . . . and let down her kingdom.

"You're welcome to stay with me as long as you like," Tabitha said. She brought the bucket of coal she had scooped to the table where Snow White was sitting and set it down, then sat across from her. "Mouse likes to drift between houses, and it's been a while since I've had a house-mate my age."

"It would be nice to stay the night, thank you. But then I need to find a way back home."

Tabitha gave her a sympathetic look. "I know it's hard,

especially since you've only just arrived. But it'll be much easier if you settle into the idea that this is your home now."

"Oh, no, I can't do that. My kingdom needs me."

"Your kingdom might have to recruit someone else for help, Snow White."

Tabitha didn't say it maliciously, but Snow White couldn't even think of that as a possibility. It was her kingdom. Her responsibility.

Tabitha looked at her freshly washed hands, then brushed coal dust from them. "So, how did you end up here?"

Snow White suspected this was a topic she would be talking about with everyone she met.

"I was in her way," Snow White said, realizing a second later it was a different answer from the one she had given to Henry. But perhaps a more accurate one.

"Oh, wow," said Tabitha. "That's almost the same thing that happened to me. Except *she* got in *my* way, causing me to step on the hem of her dress. I didn't even make her trip, but I suppose she takes the end of her dress that drags in the dirt *very seriously*."

Snow White had never heard something that was so ridiculous and horrifying at once, and her mind was unsure which way to lean.

But then Tabitha burst out laughing, and it made Snow White smile.

"Your water has gone cold?" she asked, recovering from her laughter.

Snow White looked down at her feet; she had not even realized she had removed them from the water. "Yes, and they feel much better."

"Good. Then let me show you to your room." Tabitha held the bucket in both arms and led Snow White around the corner to another room, similar in size to the one they had just been in. There was a small stone heater in the corner, and Tabitha crouched down and began filling it with coal from her bucket. "It tends to get chilly at night here, so if you feel yourself getting a little cold, you can light this. Or fill the warmer over there and put it at the foot of your bed."

"Thank you," said Snow White. Then, because the question had been pulling on her, she asked, "Are you sure there's no possible way back?"

Tabitha sighed. "Well . . . if you really want to know: there are two ways back. Well . . . *supposedly*. The first is true love's kiss."

Snow White scrunched her nose. It was romantic, to be sure, but impossible given their state of enchanted sleep.

Tabitha snorted. "Trust me, we all know how far-fetched it sounds."

"What is the other way?" Snow White asked.

Tabitha chewed on the nail of her pointer finger for a moment. "According to legend, Diamant was created when the Queen was very young and still learning to master her skills. She didn't yet understand the rules of magic or that every spell requires balance."

"Balance?" Snow White wondered aloud.

"That's right. Even though the Queen wanted to create an evil place, good magic still exists. That's why the Ruby Heart is here—an object that can grant a wish to return home."

Snow White gasped. "So there *is* good magic in this world." She had known it! She had known there must be a way to return home. Where there was a problem, there was always a solution.

"There has to be," said Tabitha. "As I said, spells require balance. The Queen only wanted wickedness in her world, but because she refused to compromise anything for it, the magic made those compromises for her—good to balance her evil."

"That's so amazing. It's like a little bit of hope in the midst of darkness."

Tabitha shrugged. "I don't know about that. Because as you can imagine, the Queen was furious when she realized what the Ruby Heart could do. She intended to destroy it, and all shreds of hope with it. But every time she tried, her efforts drained her magic and she only managed to break off a few tiny pieces. For that reason—or so the legend says—instead of trying to destroy it, she simply made it nearly impossible to reach. Not only are there three trials to be won, but also she has enchanted the land with traps. Not to mention all the creatures in this land are servants to her. They reflect her wicked intent."

Snow White did not need to be reminded of her earlier encounter. If that was just the beginning of what she would face . . . She shuddered at the thought.

Still . . . "Good magic will always triumph over evil," said Snow White. "The Ruby Heart will work. I'm sure of it."

Tabitha looked at her with a bit of concern. "Oh, Snow White . . . these are all just legends, you know. I don't think there's an actual way out of here. Unless the Queen dies, maybe." She brushed more coal dust from her hands. "It's nearly nightfall now, and I'm sure you're tired. I'll leave you to rest."

Snow White wanted to ask more questions . . . but if Tabitha didn't believe in the legends, perhaps she wasn't the one to ask for more specifics. Besides, it had been a long day, and she was a bit tired. "Thank you for everything, Tabitha."

"It's no trouble at all," Tabitha said, smiling, as she left the room. "Good night, Snow White."

"Good night."

Snow White looked around the room. The sound of a hammer on a chisel caught her attention from outside. She peered through the small window. The houses were all so close together, but there seemed to be an open area cleared, with something like a furnace in the space. It cast orange light on the dark houses surrounding it.

There was a worktable, as well, with a man sitting there, carving away at something. Partly lit by the furnace and partially shadowed, he was crafting some sort of tool out of a hard gemstone. So that was where Tabitha's pickaxe and Henry's sword had come from. Snow White supposed it was silly to think those things just existed here, but she hadn't imagined someone would have to construct them. It was fascinating to watch.

But it wasn't until she saw Tabitha walk out with a steaming bowl—the one she had soaked her feet in—that Snow White realized the man working was Henry. When he and Tabitha were next to each other, even lit by only the furnace, it was clearer than ever that they were related. Now that Snow White was really looking, she noticed that they were even close to the same height. Yet at the same time, they were complete opposites. Tabitha was the sun to Henry's storm cloud.

It looked as though Tabitha was chiding him for something. He rubbed the back of his neck nervously as a smile formed on his lips. It was nice seeing them together. Snow White was an only child, but she imagined it was a special thing to have someone love you unconditionally—even if siblings did seem to give each other a hard time and tease each other often. Suddenly, Henry looked up and caught Snow White's gaze. She closed the blinds quickly and took a breath. A blush of embarrassment spread across her cheeks. She shouldn't have been observing them. "Time for bed," she murmured.

She winced as she plopped down too quickly on the smoothed stone bed. She bundled up her skirt beneath her to act as a cushion as she lay down on her side. This place was going to take a lot of getting used to.

And even while thinking that, Snow White realized that part of her still could not fathom that she was there, in

Diamant. In a world the Queen had created, made of nothing but gemstones of all kinds, cruel even in their beauty. It was strange and vicious, and she didn't want to think about it. Still, she had to. . . . She had to acknowledge everything to find a way out.

She took hold of the locket she wore and immediately thought of her father. What would he do in a situation like this? She wasn't nearly as fair, brave, and true as he was, but she knew he would do all he could to get home. He wouldn't just lie there, waiting, while his friends and kingdom were in danger.

But she was not her father, and she wasn't sure she ever could be. Not with the odds as stacked against her as they were.

Still, she had to try.

The Ruby Heart might very well be a legend, but at that moment it was the only hope Snow White had of getting home. The idea of trials terrified her, because she knew that if the Queen had anything to do with them, they would be just as awful as the wolf. But sometimes the hardest things were the most important, and Snow White had to do everything she could to get home and protect her friends from whatever the Queen was planning next.

But for the moment, she needed sleep. She would have

the following day, when her body was rested and her mind was clear, to decide her next move. Maybe then she would know what to do. The long walk to town had done her in, and with the nice warm coals keeping her cozy, she found her way to sleep.

4

*S*now White slipped into one of those dreams where one knew they were dreaming but couldn't do much about it. She knew because she was kneeling across from Jonathan, the charming thief who had saved her life—and she his—on more than one occasion. And even as she reminded herself it was a dream, she touched his light brown hair, needing more than anything to see if he was real. And lo and behold, his hair felt like hair. He even smelled like home, like grass and cedar and other natural things. Natural things that she would never find in the world of Diamant.

At the thought of where she was, she saw a bright

orange light. She and Jonathan both leapt to their feet. In the distance stood Snow White's kingdom . . . in flames. The fire burned like the sun, violently hot and bright, licking the sky as it billowed black smoke.

And in that soot-filled smoke was a pair of glowing brown eyes, like the color of a smoky quartz.

"You can't protect your kingdom from me," the Queen's voice screeched from the cloud of smoke. "You can't even protect your little thief."

Snow White's heart dropped, and when she turned to look at Jonathan, he was no longer real, made of flesh and bone. Instead he was motionless, frozen in his stance, looking at Snow White's kingdom burning . . . his body made completely of solid diamond. Not like the wolves of Diamant, who had functioning organs, who could move and breathe and growl. Jonathan was nothing but a statue. No more.

The Queen laughed at her little trick. It was a wicked, heartless sound that sent chills running through Snow White's bones.

"Foolish little girl," the Queen crowed. "You can't even save yourself."

And suddenly, gems began encasing her feet and crawling up her body with violent snaps as they grew and

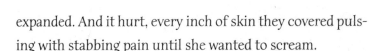

expanded. And it hurt, every inch of skin they covered pulsing with stabbing pain until she wanted to scream.

"This is a dream," Snow White said, but she couldn't wake up no matter how hard she fought to alert her body. "It's just a dream—"

The gems went from crawling to consuming, clawing up her body, all over her, with vicious intent, swallowing her whole—

A small tapping on Snow White's shoulder jolted her from an uneven sleep, from her nightmare. Her eyes flew open as she panicked, for a moment imagining a figure far more terrifying than the wolf—and she was not sure if she was seeing someone or some sort of specter. What a strange, alarming experience, to be awakened by someone standing over one's bed.

But as her eyes adjusted, she realized it was the little girl, Mouse, standing over her.

"Oh." Snow White rubbed her eyes, hiding her relief behind her hand. No monsters made of gems or specters. Not even the Queen. Just a curious little girl. "What's wrong, Mouse? Can't you sleep?"

The girl plopped down on the bed unceremoniously; she must have been used to sleeping on the stone, because she showed no sign of discomfort. "I heard you talking to

Tabitha today. How upset you were about your kingdom. Sorry you can't go home to them."

Snow White was slightly shocked to hear the girl's voice—which, she supposed, was an odd reaction, because just because someone didn't speak didn't mean they couldn't. "Thank you. That's sweet of you to say."

"I don't want you to be sad anymore. So I think you really need to see something, now."

"At this hour?" Snow White yawned. She wasn't keen on trying to go back to sleep again and possibly falling back into another nightmare, but the thought of going out into the night in a world she didn't know all the rules of yet wasn't a thrilling alternative. She had learned quickly not to underestimate the place. "I could better see it by daylight, I'm sure."

"But it only happens at night." Mouse shook Snow White's shoulder, then hopped up and bounced on her toes. "And it doesn't happen every night. Hurry, we don't want to miss it."

She grabbed Snow White's arm and pulled, giving her no choice but to follow.

"You'll feel so much better once you see," Mouse said, leading Snow White outside. The night was slightly chilly, and Snow White missed the coals at her feet. She and the girl wove around the houses, all of them dark and still sleeping. Even the furnace Henry had been working beside earlier lay dormant, not even embers remaining in the coals. Night there didn't sound like night back home; there were no frog croaks or cricket chirps, no birdcalls through trees with *actual* leaves. If Snow White listened very closely, she could hear water trickling in the well until they were far from the town square. But other than that, and the noises she and Mouse created as they walked, it was dead silent.

They were still technically inside the walls when the houses turned back along a path surrounded by trees, allowing the townspeople to enjoy the experience of the woods without leaving the protection of the wall. And it was then that Snow White heard . . . music?

Ahead, it looked like there was golden lantern light, but other colors were there as well, that same stained glass effect Snow White had seen with the leaves. Shadows, ghostly but full of verve and life, danced against the light.

As soon as she saw it, Mouse exclaimed, "There it is!" and pulled Snow White on faster. The closer they got, the louder the atmosphere became, until Snow White was swallowed by the jolly sounds of laughter and singing. As soon as she made it to the edge of the trees, Snow White stopped, leaning a hand on one of the trunks to catch the breath she had just lost at the sight of it all.

The sky was illuminated by strings of lanterns hung from trees to poles in a chaotic array, so plentiful and bright they blocked out the natural stars. Underneath was a square dance floor, where about three dozen people who refused to sleep were dancing the night away. Tables full of people focusing on their own crafts or clapping along to the music surrounded the dancing. Everyone looked happy to be there and excited for the festivities.

Snow White couldn't help smiling as she looked down at Mouse. "How wonderful!" she exclaimed loudly enough to be heard over the music.

Mouse beamed up at her. "Let's go have some fun!"

The two of them rushed down a slight hill to join the party. There were a few people playing instruments, and for a moment Snow White stood and watched them strum their gutstring guitars and beat a lively rhythm on hand drums. She longed to join in the dancing, but Mouse wanted to show her everything first, so she pulled Snow White to a table where others were making jewelry and crafts out of sparkling stones.

"See?" said Mouse. "There's a little bit of fun for everyone."

Snow White ran her fingers along one of the finished pieces—a necklace made of sapphires. "It's all so beautiful."

"And over there they're playing games," said Mouse, pointing. "What do you want to do first?"

What a decision! There were so many activities going on, with almost the feel of a carnival or fair. But she saw the way Mouse's eyes kept darting back to the table with jewels.

"How about jewelry making?" Snow White suggested.

"Yeah!" Mouse said so enthusiastically that Snow White had to smile.

Snow White supposed it would be nice to do something that would last . . . something she could take with her to remember the night by. The few sitting there welcomed them excitedly, giving them space on the benches to sit.

Snow White had made jewelry when she was younger, out of paper and cloth or string and beads. But never in her life had she ever strung together real gemstones. The small pieces had been predrilled so that all she had to do was string the provided twine through. There were bright blue sapphires, opals the gentle blue of eggshells, stones as turquoise as the sea or as flaming gold as topaz. But when Snow White saw the pearls, she knew they were the only ones she wanted. She took one into her palm to admire it, watching it glow in the surrounding light. It was simple and small, with an understated, iridescent beauty. It reminded her of her mother.

Across the table from her, Mouse was stringing her gems haphazardly, with no rhyme or reason to the colors or patterns. But when Snow White began stringing her pearls, she did so carefully, lovingly. Part of her felt that this necklace was important—that it was more than just a beautiful thing to keep with her. That, in a way, it was a memory in itself.

"Look at mine, Snow White!" Mouse exclaimed, holding up her array of mismatched gems by both ends of the twine it was strung across.

"It's beautiful!"

"Can you tie it for me?" Mouse held out the two ends to Snow White without waiting for an answer, but Snow White was happy to help. The little girl turned so her back faced Snow White, and she barely allowed her to tie a knot before leaping off the table. "Ready to play some games?"

"I'm not quite finished with my necklace."

"What's taking so long?" Mouse groaned, sagging her body. "Hurry, we're going to miss everything!"

"There's no sense in your waiting to have fun," said

Snow White, grinning at the little girl's enthusiasm. "I'll meet you after I'm done."

"Okay!" That arrangement seemed to make Mouse feel better, because she immediately popped up from her floppy state. "See you over at the horseshoes. I'll be playing it for hours!"

Mouse raced off, and Snow White shook her head and returned her attention to her project. She took her time, even though Mouse was waiting. Mouse was occupied, anyway, and one could not rush joy. Snow White strung the pearls, filling the strand. The more pearls she added, the more comforted she felt. She had not left much room to knot the ends, but she managed to double tie them.

Finally, it was finished. Snow White put the necklace on over her head, then looked around to find a mirror so she could admire it. Luckily, there was one on a nearby pole. Snow White watched her reflection touch the pearls. They were indeed lovely, but Snow White suddenly wondered if they would cease to exist after she awoke.

Don't be silly, she thought. *They're only in your mind, after all.*

"Why, if it isn't our new little stardrop," someone behind her said. Snow White turned around to see Henry approaching. His arms were spread in greeting, and a genuine smile stretched his cheeks. "Welcome to the party."

"What's gotten into you, Henry?" Snow White asked, eyeing him curiously. Even though she'd known him for only half a day, it seemed more than enough time to judge his character. And Snow White had never seen him so happy.

"I haven't a clue what you mean," Henry replied, crossing his arms and giving her a sly look.

And now he was teasing her good-naturedly? Oh, this was *not* the boy she'd just traveled with earlier that day. "Is it really you, Henry? Or do you have a twin brother who's been scowling at me all day?"

"I can certainly continue to scowl if that will make you feel more comfortable."

Snow White chuckled. "You're right. Perhaps instead of asking questions, I should just enjoy it."

Henry's grin grew. "Since you're so curious, I'll let you in on a secret, Stardrop." He pulled a smooth stone from his pocket and tossed it to her. "Have a look."

Snow White caught it and turned it in her hands, searching for . . . she wasn't sure what. Special markings? Writing? It looked like an ordinary stone, though she supposed in a place made of gems that was an extraordinary thing in itself. "What is it?"

"A Forgetting Stone," Henry said. He'd strolled over to her and peered over her shoulder to watch her further scrutinize the object.

"How does it work?" she asked.

Henry reached over and plucked the stone from her fingers, then stuffed it into his pocket. "You can wish to forget any one thing, and as long as the moon is up, it will be forgotten."

"And when the sun comes up?"

Henry shrugged with a sad sort of sigh. "Nothing lasts forever."

"What good is forgetting one thing for just a night?" Snow White wondered aloud.

"You yourself said I'm different than I was earlier." Henry grinned, pleased. "Come, let's dance."

Snow White couldn't help smiling. Perhaps it did make a difference. The Henry she had met earlier would never have danced, let alone smiled that much. But one small thought still pulled at the back of her laughter: what could he have chosen to forget? "I would never have imagined that you dance, Henry."

He gave her a look of mock offense. "You speak out of turn, Princess. I am *the best* dancer in all of Diamant."

"Well, in that case . . ." Snow White giggled as Henry

pulled her onto the dance floor just in time for another fast and lively jig to begin.

It wasn't a dance she was familiar with, but the movements were simple—a turn here, a kick there—and soon Snow White was jigging along with everyone as if she had been doing it all her life. They threw their hands up in the air, clapped, and stomped to the beat. It was exhilarating, the breeze rushing through her short black hair as she spun, her excitement from the rhythm sending joy sprinting through her. They danced until they were stumbling away from the dance floor from too much spinning, laughing together.

They collapsed onto their backs on a soft patch of ground near the trees, away from the crowd. There it was dim and cool and soothing after all that activity, with the hanging lanterns like burning stars overhead.

"That was so much fun," Snow White panted, gazing up at the beautiful view.

"And we will do it again in a couple of days," Henry replied, resting an arm behind his head to cushion it. "Something to look forward to."

Snow White shifted onto her stomach and leaned on her elbows so she could look at him. She had never seen him so relaxed before. Granted, she had met him just that morning, but even through all those hours of travel, she had seen only one side to him. This was an entirely different Henry from the one who had found her on the path and led her to Diamant. That night he wasn't carrying himself like he was some palace guard with the weight of the world on his shoulders. That night she was reminded that he was just a boy. Because he truly looked like one.

His brown eyes moved from the sky to her, and he raised his brows. "Have I grown a second nose or something? Why are you looking at me like that?"

"I was just thinking . . ." Snow White said. "Henry?"

"Hmm?"

"What did you wish to forget?" She found herself whispering the question. It seemed so personal, yet she couldn't tamp down her desire to know.

He looked at her as if he didn't understand the question. "I don't remember. And I hope I never do. Life is so joyful without it, whatever it was." He yawned and closed his eyes.

Yes, of course. While the moon was still in the sky, he would never remember the one thing he'd wished away. Yet Snow White felt sadness for him, for the pain he couldn't remember. The very fact that he *needed* to forget in order to be happy hurt her heart.

"I want you to have this." She removed her necklace and scooted even closer to him to lay the pearls around his neck. "I thought of my family when I made this. I hope that when you wear it and look at it, you can feel that peaceful joy of home, too."

He opened his eyes and lifted the gift to look at it. "Aww, Stardrop. It's you. They're literally snow white." His eyes fluttered shut again as he appeared to be overcome by true sleepiness only happiness could bring on. "I can feel it," he said.

"Wait a moment," said Snow White, giggling a little. She patted Henry's shoulder, but he simply sighed without opening his eyes. "Silly boy, are you really going to sleep here? Let me walk you home."

"Too tired . . ." He yawned. "I'll walk you home tomorrow. . . ."

Snow White shook her head. It was endearing, but there was no way she could allow him to sleep there on the ground all night. But as she wasn't leaving the party quite yet, there was no harm in allowing him to rest there a moment. Besides, all that dancing had taken a lot out of her, too, in the best way.

For a moment they were silent, and only the sound of Henry's steady breathing filled the space between them.

"Can I tell you another secret, Stardrop?" he asked suddenly, his voice barely a whisper.

"More secrets, Henry?" Snow White asked, grinning. "What more could there possibly be?"

"I just want to say that . . . princesses . . . aren't so bad."

"Well, I appreciate the change of heart," she replied. She waited for a response, but there was nothing except for a contented sigh. "Henry?"

"Snow White?"

She turned to see Tabitha approaching from the magical dimness of the trees. "Oh, hello," she said as she got up and dusted off her dress.

"I didn't expect to see you here tonight," Tabitha said, surprise flickering in her eyes. "I thought perhaps you'd be too tired from your long journey."

"Yes, well, Mouse insisted," Snow White said. "What about you? Are you enjoying the party?"

Tabitha's eyes went straight to Henry's sleeping form. "I'm just here for collection duty, I'm afraid. He'd never make it back to his bed without me."

"I can help you if you'd like," said Snow White.

But Tabitha had already hoisted Henry onto his feet with ease. She had looked strong but apparently was even stronger than Snow had expected. "It's no problem," she said, slinging Henry's arm over her shoulder. "I do this so often it's become part of my routine." She smiled. "Go on and enjoy your first Diamant party. You deserve a little fun."

Henry mumbled something incoherent before Tabitha led him away.

For a moment Snow White watched them go as she considered whether to follow Tabitha's suggestion or find her own bed.

But she had promised she would join Mouse. Although, the little girl seemed distracted enough—and most definitely had not been exaggerating when she said she could play horseshoes for hours. Snow White was plenty fatigued herself from all that dancing, though not quite sleepy yet, so she decided a short stroll would do her some good instead.

All around her, the party still raged, unaware of and unbothered by her quiet disengagement from it. Since she didn't have Mouse pulling her quickly along, she took in everything at a casual pace, weaving through the trees as she kept to the edges. The dance floor was still as lively as ever, the craft tables still full.

She turned to walk away from the ruckus and kept on distancing herself from it until the music's blaring lessened, and she could hear herself think. Until she could smell the night. It smelled different there than at home. In the real world, there were plants and animals to add their specific scents to the air, not to mention the smells of food cooking, depending on where she was. In Diamant it smelled of earth, but in a less varied, less obvious way. Because the beautiful part of smelling the outdoors was that it was *alive*. Here everything might have looked exquisite, but it didn't smell like life.

Snow White suddenly tripped to a stop, her heart racing as she saw movement among the trees. But it was silly to panic; she was safe inside the town's walls now. No wolves could get in . . . could they?

"Hello?" she said—an incredibly silly reaction if it actually *was* a wolf, as that would just alert it to her location and make eating her easier.

But instead, a woman replied, "Yes? Who's there?"

Snow White sighed in relief. "I didn't mean to disturb you," she said, rounding a tree to see an older woman sitting on a stump. But she froze when she saw the glint of tears on the woman's face.

Seeing Snow White, the woman wiped at her eyes quickly. "Oh. You're the new stardrop?"

"Yes."

"What can I help you with, my dear?"

Snow White hesitated. "Nothing, ma'am. Thank you."

"I saw you dancing with Henry out there. I suppose Tabitha has already come for him. He likes to dance himself into a coma." The woman tried to smile a little, although it was hard to hide that she had been crying with her puffy eyes and sniffling.

"I don't mean to pry, ma'am, but . . . are you all right?" Snow White asked.

"Oh," the woman said, wiping her eyes again as fresh tears began to crest over her lids. "Just missing my husband, that's all." She held up her locket, and Snow White walked over and sat beside her to better see it. The man in the locket-sized painting had dark hair, and although his mustache blocked his lips, his eyes gave him a kind expression. "We've been married ten years. Or at least we would be if I wasn't . . ."

She didn't need to finish the sentence.

"What happened to cause you to end up here?" Snow White asked.

"The Queen came to purchase a horse from our farm. She didn't like the price and wasn't willing to negotiate." She wiped more stray tears. "So for the past year, all I've had is the painting in this locket to remember him by. Such a handsome man, isn't he? I wonder if he waited."

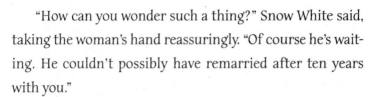

"How can you wonder such a thing?" Snow White said, taking the woman's hand reassuringly. "Of course he's waiting. He couldn't possibly have remarried after ten years with you."

"People do."

"But not if their spouse is stuck in a cursed sleep. He loves you too much for that. I'm sure of it."

"Oh . . . how young and sweet you are," the woman said, patting Snow White's hand. Her tone wasn't condescending but full of doubts and bitterness and regret. Longing and loss. She sniffled and gave Snow White's hand back to her. "Don't mind me. I think I am just a little overtired, that's all. Go on and enjoy the party, dear." And she stood and walked away toward the town.

Snow White remained sitting for a moment, an uneasiness clouding her mind. In the middle of a celebration, people were mourning their lives lost. First Henry, who needed a magic stone to erase a memory for the night. Now this woman, who had been there an entire year and had not stopped longing for her husband. And who knew how many others were just like them—just like Snow White. Who had not forgotten, no matter how long they had been there. Who were still mourning the loss of the lives they had once had. It seemed too cruel an existence to bear.

But somehow, it gave her hope. She wasn't the only one who felt lost and discontented in Diamant. She wasn't alone.

"There you are!" Mouse ran over and grabbed Snow White by the hand. "Aren't you having fun?"

"Yes," Snow White replied, despite all the thoughts spinning in her head. "I think I'm just a little tired from my journey."

Mouse drooped a little, clearly disappointed that Snow White wasn't up for more games. "It does take a while to adjust to being stardropped. We can go home now if you want." She shuffled a little. "I just wanted to show you that this place isn't all bad. Maybe out there, beyond the wall, but not in this little town we created." She laced her fingers, squeezing her hands together. "This place has been my home for a long time, and if I never settled in and accepted it, I would've never found happiness." She gestured to the party with a smile. "None of us would have."

Snow White nodded, absorbing her words. There was joy to be found anywhere if one knew where to look for it.

But outside the walls, it wasn't as kind, and as someone who had lived half of her childhood contained and alone, she would not wish a life behind walls on anyone. Besides, it was clear not everyone was happy living a life that wasn't theirs. That night, a night that had been meant to expel Snow White's worries and fears of the future, had done nothing but proved it.

As beautiful as it could be, the place had the makings of a nightmare—the promises of a dream that was nothing but unnatural and wrong. The people there were like birds caught in cages when they should have the entire sky.

And Snow White had every intention of soaring.

There had not been many hours of sleep left when Snow White made it back to her room. Yet when morning dawned, she was wide awake as soon as her eyes opened. Her mind was perfectly clear, as if she was continuing the last thought she had had the night before without the break of sleep in between. Unfortunately, she also awakened to pain, and she winced as she tried to rise. She had slept well and deeply after all that dancing, so she had not shifted, and her back was feeling the effects of lying on the stone slab without moving all night. But it wasn't anything a few quick stretches couldn't fix.

Snow White and Mouse had parted ways for a while after their talk the night before so that Mouse could play more games. She didn't remember Mouse returning, but Mouse must have found her way home sometime after Snow White had fallen asleep, and curled into the bed beside her. Mouse's dark hair was wildly out of place, even a little matted in spots. She was on her side, knees pressed up to her elbows. She snored quietly, her mouth opened the smallest bit. Something about the scene reminded Snow White of a content kitten.

Snow White winced as she turned to look up at the glittering ceiling, but she had more important things to worry about than a little stiffness. It was time to focus on the mission for the day. She didn't have to ask herself any more questions. She had made up her mind.

This place—though some accepted it as their new home—was not real. Nothing but a cruel enchantment. There was no way she could stay there, not when her life, her friends, her kingdom were all on the other side.

She could not abandon her people. She would not.

And perhaps . . .

She looked at Mouse, sleeping soundly. She thought of how Henry had been the night before, so vulnerable. Perhaps she could help more than just herself. Perhaps there was a way to get this dear little girl home, too. Her and Henry and Tabitha. And everyone else in Diamant.

She got up carefully, so as not to wake Mouse, and tip-toed outside.

There were the sounds of the bustle of people up and about, even if Snow White could not see them around the narrow alleyways. She stepped out from between two houses, but perhaps she should have looked first, because she nearly knocked right into Henry.

"Oh—Good morning, Henry." Snow White felt fondness grow in her heart as she remembered the previous night, all the merrymaking, the way they had danced the night away. What a wonderful memory to keep with her of her first night in Diamant.

"Can you not speak so loudly this early, Stardrop?" he said. He had his sword at his hip and a pickaxe in his gloved hand. That seemed like an awful lot of sharp objects for one person to be carrying. "Your voice is high and I have a headache."

She blinked at his tone. Yes . . . of course. She supposed she had hoped a little bit of joy would remain in Henry, but the sun was up, which meant the Forgetting Stone was no longer functioning. This was the true him, then, not the smiling, joyful boy she'd danced and laughed with the previous night. And Snow White was disappointed to see that he wasn't wearing the necklace she had given him the night before . . . as if the gesture had meant nothing to him at all.

Snow White resisted the urge to demand the necklace back. Instead, she responded with, "You should be kinder to people."

He paused and frowned at her, as if no one had ever told him that before. "As I said, I have a headache," he said, his tone softer this time.

It wasn't an apology, but it was progress.

He walked on, and Snow White followed.

"When does everyone usually wake up here?" she asked.

"Whenever they want."

Snow White huffed. "I was going to make an announcement in the square, but I may need to go door-to-door and tell people personally instead."

Henry glanced over his shoulder at her. "Don't do that."

"Well, can you lead me to the town square, then?"

"I'm headed there now. Tabitha forgot her pickaxe."

"That's very kind of you."

He shrugged. "She brings me rock salt at the end of a long day. I fetch her things even when they're all the way across town. It's not so much kindness as sibling loyalty."

"That is a sort of kindness, in a way."

"I would never do that for a stranger," he said with a bit of a scoff. "Is it still kindness, then?"

"In that case, I suppose you do it out of love."

He said nothing and kept walking—and since there was no protest, Snow White continued to follow.

"So why does Tabitha need her pickaxe?" she asked, if only to change the subject.

"To fix the well," he said. He seemed relieved that they had moved on. "To break up some stones to fill in a few holes."

"Does it not work if there are holes?"

"You never run out of questions." He gave her a slightly irritated look. "It works the same. The repairs are just for aesthetics."

"She must enjoy what she does very much."

"I think you'll find, Stardrop, that enjoyment is not a requirement for most of the things people do around here. If it isn't done for survival or entertainment, it's usually done out of boredom. People need things to do here so they don't feel so lost and useless."

"And can the same be said for you?" Snow White asked.

He huffed, and Snow White noticed he was walking a bit faster. The previous night he had been all smiles, and that day he was having none of it. She rushed to catch up with him.

"What about when you rescued me?" she asked. "You didn't risk your life out of the kindness of your heart, I suppose?"

"That's quite enough questions for one morning."

Snow White frowned. "It's an easy one. And anyway, I deserve to know."

He huffed again. "It was something to do."

"I think you're being dishonest, Henry. You could have left me out in the woods to wander alone, but instead you helped me. I don't think you would have put yourself in danger like that if it was just 'something to do.'"

He gave her a scrutinizing side-eye, and they continued the walk in silence.

When they made it to the square, there were people— including Tabitha—working on the well. Others were playing chess. A handful were just standing and chatting. The town center seemed to be the place to go for everything, so there was a decent-sized audience for what she knew she needed to do. If one or two people chose to go with her, that would be enough. If they truly wanted to go home, as she did, they would step forward.

Henry handed his sister the pickaxe, and she took it

and smiled up at him and Snow White. "What have you two been up to this morning?"

"*We* haven't been up to anything," said Henry, rolling his eyes. "She just follows me around for some reason."

"I do not *follow you around*," Snow White said with a scowl, her hands on her hips. "I just couldn't remember how to get to the town square."

"So you followed me."

"Hey, Snow White," Tabitha interrupted, glaring at her brother, "are you adjusting to everything all right?"

"Not really," she said, frowning as she watched Henry walk away from them.

"It takes time. Trust me, you'll fall into the rhythm of this place."

Snow White watched Henry exit the town center. He was swallowed by the curve of the alleyways beside the houses, and disappointment overtook her. Not just disappointment, but doubt. After how well they had gotten along the night before, she had thought maybe he would join her or, at the very least, help her convince the crowd.

She had to do this for the people who felt hopeless, like the woman she'd spoken with the night before. If she could make a difference, it was her duty to do something.

She took a deep breath and grabbed on to one of the pillars of the well, carefully stepping up onto it.

"Excuse me," she called . . . though perhaps *called* is an exaggeration. Her words must have been louder in her own head than from her lips, because no one had heard her except for a few people working on the well beneath her.

"What do you need, Snow White?" Tabitha asked.

"I just wanted everyone's attention to say something."

Tabitha put her finger and thumb in her mouth and whistled. *Loudly.* Everyone on all corners of the town square stopped what they were doing to look. "Listen up!" she called. Now *that* was a call.

"Thank you," Snow White whispered.

Tabitha nodded before going back to work.

"I've decided to go retrieve the Ruby Heart," Snow White said. "We all know it's our one reliable hope of breaking out of the enchantment the Queen has us under and going home. So I'd like to offer the opportunity to anyone who wants to join me. Together we can change our fate. We can *all* go home. Who will go with me?"

There was a broad silence. That was not the response Snow White had been expecting. She scanned the area to find the townspeople looking at one another, as if confused by what she had said. Confused or disturbed. Even Tabitha stared, stunned.

"It's just a story, sweetie," someone said, and Snow White's heart sank when she saw that it was the woman she had spoken to the night before—who had been mourning the loss of her life, her husband. She wanted to go home as badly as Snow White, and at the same time had no faith in ever getting there. In that way, she had accepted her fate.

"But what if it's true?" Snow White said. "What if there's a way to get home, and all we have to do is find it?"

"This *is* our home," someone else said.

"Why waste our time leaving the safety of the wall for nothing?" said someone else. "There are wolves out there."

"Snow White," said Tabitha, leaving her tools and standing up, her patient tone one would use when talking to a human child who thinks she's a bird, "even if the legends are all true, it's far too dangerous to go on your own . . . and most of us have had too much false hope in regard to the Ruby Heart to ever want to bother trying again."

"But if the legends are true . . ." For a moment Snow White wasn't sure what to say next. How was she to convince people who had long before given up hope? "We can't let the Queen get away with this." She was losing courage by the moment. "Will no one go with me?" she managed to say with the last of her voice.

The silence stretched longer than the first. Some turned away from her, going back to what they had been doing before she interrupted. Some looked at her with pity, some with annoyance, others with fear. No one seemed to find value in arguing with the girl who had just a day earlier fallen from the stars, who was still in denial and would soon see reason without their having to waste their breath or energy. Gradually, everyone went back about their business, ignoring Snow White completely.

"No one?" Snow White asked in barely a whisper.

"I will."

Her heart grew three sizes when she saw Henry coming through the crowd again. She had not seen him return to the square, but she was happy to know she had been right: he would help her. And together they would save everyone, even if no one else dared to come along on the journey.

"Henry," said Tabitha, grabbing his arm. "Are you sure about this? Last time resulted in nothing but disappointment."

"I'm sure," he said, sighing, as she cupped his face in her hands.

"This time will be different," said Snow White, trying to give her new friends a reassuring smile.

"I'm afraid you don't know that, Snow White." Tabitha sighed and shook her head. "But if anyone has the determination to find the Ruby Heart, it's you two."

"Thank you, Tabitha," Snow White said. She turned to Henry, feeling warm and cozy even as he scowled. "I'm so happy you agreed to come, Henry. Part of me thought you were sick of me."

The corners of his mouth curled upward, but only the slightest bit. "Someone has to keep you from petting monsters."

"Wait!" cried someone with a small voice. The adults in the crowd shifted as someone ran around them, and then Mouse ran up to the well, looking up at Snow White with hope and excitement. "I'm going with you, too."

"Children don't belong on quests," Henry said sourly.

"I'd be older than you now if this was the real world, so *mm!*" and she ended it by sticking her tongue out at him.

Snow White chuckled. "She has a point."

"If she gets hurt, it's on you," Henry replied bitterly as he made his way through the crowd.

"Where are you going?" Snow White called.

"Was your plan to walk aimlessly?" he called back. "Come along. I'm getting the map."

"Oh, no," groaned Mouse. "Not the map again."

Snow White studied the little girl's exaggerated lament, pausing to wait for her as Henry trudged ahead of them. "There's a map to the Ruby Heart?"

"Henry thinks it's magic," said Mouse with distaste. "*I* think it's rubbish!"

Snow White smiled politely at the remaining villagers who continued to stare in disbelief. "Well, we shall see, won't we?"

"Keep up," Henry said over his shoulder. The girls grinned at each other, Mouse giggling, before rushing to catch up.

They wove among the houses, back toward where the party had been held the night before. Snow White looked around, her gaze lingering on the hanging lanterns, on the spot among the trees where she and Henry had collapsed in breathless laughter. She could see why people would want to stay there, why people would be reluctant to go with her. Because behind the wall there was safety, and in time one could perhaps even forget that they belonged in the waking world instead of this one. But it wasn't their home, despite the efforts they'd gone through to make it feel like one.

If anything, it was a cage.

Henry led them to a small supply shed, though there wasn't enough room for all of them. Henry alone filled the space thoroughly, having to bend over even to fit inside. So Snow White and Mouse waited outside. Snow White peered in to watch him fill a pack with a few supplies and then pull a small box from under a shelf. From it, he removed a folded piece of parchment and brought it out to them.

"I wondered where that went," said Mouse. "You map hoarder."

"Someone tried to burn it the last time it was used. I wanted to keep it safe." He unfolded it slowly, almost reverently. "Besides, I thought you didn't think it was magic."

Mouse pouted. "I *know* it's not."

"Stardrop," said Henry, holding the map down so Snow White could see, "what do you think? Magic or not?"

Snow White touched the map, following a shimmering line with her finger as it drew its way across the parchment without any aid of a writing utensil—a line she was positive was almost *glowing* with life and magic. "It *is* magic," she said quickly with excitement. "The map actually knows where we're going. It's already showing us the path to the first trial."

"Showing us *your* path," Henry clarified. He gestured

at his gloved hands. "The first person to touch it is the one who dictates the path. I figured my path had led to nowhere so many times that we should try someone new."

Mouse crinkled her dark brows in a scowl, glaring at the map. "If following the map was so easy, someone would've come back with the Ruby Heart a long time ago. How do we even know this is the right direction?"

"It's magic, Mouse," said Henry with a heavy sigh.

"Well, I for one have never had a good experience with magic. Have you, Snow White?" she asked. "Magic is how we ended up here, so what makes you think any of the magic here means us any good?"

Mouse had a point, and it made Snow White truly consider her response for a moment. "We have to give it a chance," she said. "Perhaps the map is made from good magic like the Ruby Heart. This is the only guide we have. We have to try."

"Here." Henry held a sheathed sword out to her. It was smaller than his but just as clearly a weapon. "This one will suit you nicely."

"I can't use that." Snow White took a small step back. "I prefer to solve my problems without violence."

"That's very noble of you. But the dangers of Diamant won't care how you feel."

"I'm not comfortable with it."

Henry sighed again but lowered the arm holding the sword, with no further argument leaving his lips.

"I'll hold it for you, Snow White," Mouse piped up.

"Absolutely not," Henry said, and put the sword back where he had found it. He threw the pack over his shoulders. "By the looks of the map, if we leave now, we'll get through the first trial before sundown. Let's go."

His caring about her feelings even though they could possibly inconvenience the mission reminded her of the Henry she had danced with the night before. Both versions of Henry were worth fighting for, but it was nice to know that despite all his grumbling, he did actually respect her.

And they headed off.

Word must have gotten out that the new stardrop was attempting to find the Ruby Heart, because everyone paused to look at them as they made their way back through town and toward the front gate. People came out of their houses to stare. It could not have been such an unbelievable thing, could it? Others had tried it before. Snow White tried not to let their murmurings get into her head. She could do this, whether or not others believed she could.

Henry and Mouse didn't seem bothered. Perhaps it

was just because Henry had made the journey before and Mouse had been there so long, but Henry ignored most everyone he passed, and Mouse was so busy skipping and jumping over things that she was too distracted to look at anyone.

Even though Snow White was firm in her decision, she was still relieved when they left the scrutinizing looks of the townspeople and made it out the gate. They walked on the path, heading toward where Henry had found her the day before. It was clear they were going to be doing quite a bit of walking that day, since Snow White hadn't seen anything resembling a trial when she'd been wandering the woods. They would need to go beyond that area, which was going to take a few hours at least.

As they walked, it also became clear that Henry was not interested in any sort of conversation. He walked ahead of Snow White and Mouse, his long legs making for a quick travel pace. But Snow White didn't mind that at all. Giving Henry his space allowed her and Mouse to pass the time chatting about things without the possibility of Henry's collapsing the conversation into negativity.

"Mouse, what happened to your necklace?" Snow White asked, her curiosity getting the better of her.

Mouse's nose scrunched up a bit. "What necklace?"

Snow White hesitated. "The rainbow one. I helped you put it on last night, remember?"

The little girl thought about it for a moment, until finally her eyes lit up. "Oh, yes! That was so much fun!" And then she shrugged. "I lost it."

Snow White blinked at her. "Lost it?"

"It's okay. I'll just make another one at the next party."

"Oh." Snow White twisted her mouth in thought. Lost it? Something made of such precious stones? Well, she was only a little girl, after all. And Snow White supposed gems tended to lose a bit of their value when they could be found literally everywhere. But the fact that gems were reserved for nobles and royalty back home . . . It was clear the things that held value here were the items the Queen didn't want anyone to have.

The map, for one thing.

The Ruby Heart, for another.

But thinking of Mouse losing her necklace, Snow White realized maybe she didn't want to know after all what Henry had done with the necklace she had made and gifted him. Discovering the truth might break her heart more than being left in the dark did.

The path was just as beautiful while they traveled away from town as it had been when they had gone in. At some points, depending on the angles, the gems reflected the light brightly, nearly obscuring the path as they walked. At other times, it was like walking into a dream, lovely and full of color. Dangerous and beautiful. It was like the Queen in that way.

"Henry, where are we?" Mouse complained. "Are we almost there? We've been walking for *hours*."

"*One* hour," Henry said, tight-jawed. "And why don't you go back to town if it bothers you so much?"

"No way. I'm staying with Snow White," she said, and grabbed her newfound friend's hand.

Snow White smiled down at the little girl. "Don't worry. I'm sure it's not much farther to the first trial." But when she glanced up again, Henry was shooting her an annoyed look over his shoulder. "Or not?"

He turned back to his task without a word.

For the next hour, Snow White made it her mission to distract and entertain Mouse. They played games, naming things they saw and memorizing what the last person said until their list of items could have stretched for a page. Yet they didn't stop, not even when they finally reached a smaller footpath—which Snow White was glad of, as that jade grass was some nasty business.

"We've been traveling *all day*," Mouse fussed again. It

was still an exaggeration, but close enough to the truth that Snow White had to agree with her.

Henry ignored her complaint and pressed on. They stopped to rest a few times—very short rests, as Henry was also a stickler for making good time. It was no wonder he had led so many of the journeys before this one.

But Snow White didn't mind the distance or the time it took them to get there. She was just glad they had not crossed paths with any danger yet; perhaps the wolves hunted solitary prey and didn't bother with groups. And perhaps Tabitha had been mistaken about the number of traps; they were legends, after all, and legends did tend to be exaggerated over time. Whatever the reason, it was a small relief that despite Henry's holding on to his sword, he had yet to have an opportunity to use it.

Mouse, on the other hand, was not enjoying the length of time they'd been out on the road. She huffed, picked up a small stray gem, and threw it into the tree above her. It made a beautiful tinkling sound, like a wind chime in a steady breeze, on the way up as well as on the way down— and Snow White paused to listen. Mouse giggled as soon as the rock hit the ground, and she continued on behind Henry. But Snow White couldn't forget the beauty of what she had just heard. Not everything in the Queen's enchanted world was evil. Not all of it had to be, at least.

Snow White picked up a gem of her own and threw it into the trees, hearing the bell-like music play. But she had arched her throw instead of sending it directly up as Mouse had, so on the way down, the rock hit Henry directly on the back of the head. Snow White gasped, her hands over her mouth, as he jolted to a stop. Mouse giggled uncontrollably.

"Sorry," said Snow White with a cringe.

He scowled at her over his shoulder. "Could you *not*?"

"I'm *sorry*. I certainly didn't mean to do that." She hurried to rejoin the line. "The leaves just sound so pretty. I'll throw them behind us, how about th—*ouch!*"

Snow White grabbed the top of her head where something hard had dropped onto it. It was like when she had been hit in the head with an acorn when she was little, except far harder. Either the rock she had thrown had leapt up on its own to take revenge, or . . .

She looked down near her feet, where an emerald leaf lay on the ground. It was strange how awful she felt for knocking something so beautiful from its proper place.

"Let's keep moving," said Henry, but he had barely taken another step before another leaf fell, just missing the tip of his nose . . . and embedded itself into the ground at his feet by a sharp end.

No sooner had they looked at it than they heard the tinkle of more leaves. The shaking sound swelled into a noise, now more dissonant and foreboding.

Snow White and Henry looked at each other, dread filling Snow White's gut.

They didn't even need to say anything; they both knew what would come next. Henry tore off his pack and threw it to Snow White, who used it to shield her head. And then Henry scooped up Mouse and cradled her close to his chest, and they took off running just as a chorus of leaves began to rain down on them.

But *rain* was the wrong word entirely. *Hail* would be closer, since every leaf was hard and sharp and hurt as if it struck bone when it hit its target. They fell like a deadly house of cards, and all Snow White and Henry could do was make sure they kept in front of the shower of gems. Still they were pelted by a few that hurt enough to spur them to run faster.

Snow White led the way. She had no idea where she was going. All she knew was she had to get them out, and the noise of colliding and shattering gems pummeling the ground urged her on. As she ran, she looked ahead and saw an area where the canopy of trees opened up. They would be safe there.

"We're almost there!" Snow White shouted to her friends.

Faster and faster, the gems fell, closer and closer.

But safety was right there, right within reach—

They leapt into the clearing, with the gems nearly catching Henry's foot. They had come that close. With one final crushing crash, the gems along the tree line shattered on the ground, stabbing into it like tens of dozens of violent splinters.

The three of them lay on the ground, panting. Snow White leaned on her elbows, witnessing as the woods finished its dangerous tantrum, the deep-rooted sound and shaking of the trees shifting as soon as the last stray emerald fell. And then the woods were still. There were still plenty of leaves on the trees, as if they had not lost anything at all, but the ground was littered with the evidence. Gems stuck into the ground like tiny knives. Others had shattered into pieces and were scattered across the dirt.

"Is everyone okay?" she gasped.

"You broke the trees, Snow White," said Mouse, and the amusement in her voice told Snow White the girl was unaware of how close to death they had truly gotten.

"I agree with Mouse for once," growled Henry, rubbing his shoulder. "No more throwing rocks at enchanted trees."

"To be fair, I didn't know they would start raining on us," Snow White said, pushing herself gingerly to her feet and shaking out her skirt.

"Wish that had been the first trial," Henry added. "One less thing to worry about."

"Well, how much farther are we from the first trial?"

Henry unfolded the map and studied it for a moment. He paused, then said, "This should be it." He compared the map to what he saw before him, looking at it, then back up again. "The first trial."

"A field?" Snow White wondered aloud.

"I told you that map was useless," said Mouse, crossing her small arms.

"I'm telling you; this is it," Henry insisted. He chewed his lip. "Somewhere."

Snow White stepped close to Henry to look at the map. Sure enough, the shimmery path stopped at the field, but there was no indication of what to do. "Do we walk through it?"

"Hold on." Henry unsheathed his sword and prodded the ground in front of him with it. "Feels like earth we can walk on. But walk behind me, just in case. Only step where I step."

"What will happen if we don't?" said Mouse, but her

tone was more questioning than defiant or even nervous. Henry ignored her and cut down the high grass in front of him with his sword, crushing it with his boot to create a clear print for them to follow.

Snow White took his words to heart. She watched his steps, careful to put her foot exactly where his had been. She had never completed a trial before and wanted to make sure she followed the rules perfectly—whatever those rules might be. And despite Mouse's questions, she fell into step behind Snow White, hopping from footprint to footprint, as Henry's strides were too wide for her.

When they had made it almost halfway through the field, nothing had changed. No trial had presented itself; the grass had not even poked her with Henry cutting it down ahead of him and crushing it with each step of his boots.

It wasn't until they reached the exact center of the field that there was suddenly a familiar growl.

"Great," muttered Mouse. "This is what we get for following that stupid map."

*S*now White turned around slowly, careful not to breathe too loudly or make any sudden movements. If it was the same creature as the day before, it seemed ten times as angry, its growl amplified tenfold. But . . . no. There was no way all that noise could have been coming from one creature alone.

Snow White nearly swallowed her tongue as, sure enough, creatures rose out of the high jade grass. More and more, ten, twenty. Their eyes glowed, and the texture of their upper backs seemed like raised manes.

Henry shifted so he was between Snow White and

Mouse and the creatures. "Looks like your little wolf brought friends."

His voice was dripping with sarcasm. For a second Snow White thought about when the two of them had met, about how she had begged him not to hurt the creature. But now that she knew the wolves were made by an evil, vengeful queen, she thought perhaps his words weren't so far-fetched. Perhaps the wolves had been sent to stop them.

Or perhaps . . . *this* was the trial.

Henry shifted again at a sound behind them, but there was no shielding them with his body as more creatures rose around them.

They were surrounded. Well, almost. The path they had taken was clear, and for a moment Snow White considered running back the way they had come, even though the creatures were viciously growling at the shattered pieces of grass that littered it.

Snow White hated to admit it, but right about then, they most definitely could have used that other sword Henry had offered her.

Still, the first words out of her mouth were "Don't hurt them, Henry."

"Now's not the time for your peacemaking, Stardrop,"

he replied, wiping sweat from his hands. He took a deep breath and lunged into an attack.

Snow White wouldn't tell him not to fight. Still, she cringed at the impact of his sword against gemstone, because they were not objects but living creatures. Even if they had been sent by the Queen, they couldn't have been completely evil. This wasn't their fault . . . this couldn't have been their fault.

"We're going to die!" Mouse lamented, clinging to Snow White as Henry fought off the creatures. But he barely knocked one away before two charged forward to take its place. This wasn't working, and there was no way Henry could do it alone. She hated standing by and being of no use.

And then she saw it.

The pathway they had cleared on their way there was just that: *clear*. Not a wolf in sight. And Snow White suddenly remembered when she had first awakened in Diamant and that lone wolf had come prowling and frightened her to the ground. It had just looked at the grass she had crushed then, growling at it but never touching it. Could they not step on the broken gems?

Anyway, the reason didn't matter. What mattered was that there was a way to hold them back, if only long enough to give Snow White and her friends time to think of a better plan.

"The path, Henry!" Snow White exclaimed. "They won't go in the flattened grass."

She barely saw him glance at the empty path before he began cutting the grass around him and crushing it under his boot. Snow White followed, stomping on the places he had, until they had a circle of safety around them.

"Quick thinking," he said. "Now I can just continue cutting us a path and we'll be out of here."

"It's a trial, Henry," said Snow White. "I don't think we're meant to just escape."

"Why are you overcomplicating it?" Henry said with a scowl. "They can't be killed, so it's clear the trial is to find a way out alive."

"I'm with Henry," said Mouse, tugging on Snow White's arm nervously. "Once we're out of the field, we'll be safe."

Looking around at the sea of monsters, Snow White chewed on her lip. "I've never met a living thing who was angry for no reason. Something must be terribly wrong to make them act this way."

"What's wrong is that they're wild beasts," said Henry. "They don't need a reason to attack."

"No, I mean it. Something's wrong."

"What's wrong is they want to eat us!" cried Mouse, clinging tighter to Snow White.

"There must be another way, Henry. A better way..." She prompted him to lower his sword. "Just let me try something."

Snow White approached the edge of the circle slowly, with her hand outstretched. "Don't be afraid, sweet one," she said gently to the creature closest to her, even as it growled and snapped.

Henry snatched her hand back. "Remember what happened last time you tried that?" he chastised, clearly on edge.

"Trust me," she said.

She crept closer to the wolf in front of her with her hand outstretched. Closer and closer... And just as slowly, the wolf's growl changed, dropping away and morphing into a hopeless whimper. Snow White took a breath and then ventured closer, touching the wolf's snout, and it allowed her to.

"Tell me what's wrong," she whispered. She ran her hand along the creature's snout, its head, and its cheek until the poor thing curled into her, showing her its back.

And Snow White saw it at the center of the wolf's back:

a small piece of gem that wasn't smooth and connected to the wolf's body, but sticking out of it. Poking *into* it.

Snow White pinched the small, thin gem with her fingers, resting her other hand on the back of the creature to soothe it as she yanked the invading gem free. The wolf whined a little as Snow White stroked its back slowly, looking at the item in her hand. It was no bigger than a thorn, and as sharp as one, too.

"You couldn't reach that, could you?" Snow White murmured. "How unfair."

And then the creature did a remarkable thing. It lay down at Snow White's feet, its tail wagging slowly.

"Black cauldrons . . ." Henry swore.

"How did you do that?" asked Mouse, looking shocked.

Snow White turned around and held up the thorn. "If someone's angry," she said, "there's always a reason." She looked at the sea of growling wolves. "Speak gently and move slowly. We can help them all if we're patient."

Henry and Mouse hesitated, watching as Snow White carefully and peacefully approached another wolf and removed the diamond thorn from its back. Only after seeing it work twice did Henry put his sword away and join in.

"Don't bite me," he murmured to the wolf, reaching

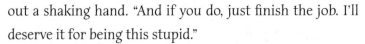

out a shaking hand. "And if you do, just finish the job. I'll deserve it for being this stupid."

"Animals can sense nerves," said Snow White.

"Such reassuring news." He plucked the thorn from the wolf quickly, a heavy exhale of relief escaping him. "Wish it made me feel better."

"See? You did it." She grinned as he shot her an unamused glare. "You're your most confident when you're being grumpy. I think that helps."

"Glad to be useful," he grumbled, moving on to the next wolf.

Snow White looked over her shoulder, and she noticed Mouse keeping her distance, still looking on in shock.

"It's okay, Mouse," Snow White called to her, but the little girl shook her head vehemently and stayed put.

Henry mumbled something under his breath, jerking his hand away as the creature he was trying to woo snapped at him.

And they continued on.

It was a slow task. Some creatures were more reluctant, more combative than others. And there were at least thirty of them to take care of, and only Snow White and Henry and their two hands to do it. Each creature they freed would either lie in the grass, docile, or run off. They kept at it until late in the afternoon, when all the wolves were feeling much better—physically and emotionally. Only then did Mouse dash to them, although she hid herself behind Snow White's skirts.

Henry seemed drained by the whole experience. He dropped to his knees, taking a heavy breath. "I knew it was going to be a trial, but I've never seen anything like *that*."

"Not all problems can be solved with a sword," Snow White said with the slightest smile. "Fairness and kindness usually do the trick just as well, if not better."

"That *was* kind," Henry agreed, with a bit of awe in his tone. Then he looked away quickly, occupying himself with taking the map from his pocket, as if he didn't want to acknowledge that the unconventional method had worked so well. "Still prefer a sword in a fight, though."

"Are you sure you don't want to try it my way first next time?"

"And risk potential death again? Pass." He unfolded the map. Stared at it. Squinted at it. "Well, look at that."

"What? What?" Mouse demanded as only a child could, jumping to see.

Henry held the map lower, and Snow White and Mouse gathered beside him. In shimmering calligraphy, the word

Fair was printed on the field where they stood, and a glittery path was marked, ending at a second location.

"The second trial," Snow White said with a gasp. "How wonderful that the magic knows exactly where to take us."

"I wish it would just take us to the Ruby Heart," murmured Mouse.

"We have to prove ourselves to earn something so precious," Henry said. He led them forward on the path marked on the map.

Snow White and Mouse exchanged amused looks. Henry's belief in the map, despite his outward disdain for everything else, was endearing.

"What?" he asked, noticing their looks.

Snow White and Mouse giggled in response.

Henry rolled his eyes. "Let's hope this next trial involves fewer things that want to eat us."

They left the field behind quickly—and justifiably so—lest the wolves change their minds about the thorns and choose the side of the Queen again, a fear Mouse had expressed a few times despite Snow White's insistence that it was unlikely. And soon they found their way back onto the walking path, which continued on the other side. Henry still led the way, walking briskly, occasionally looking at the map, not really talking much. But Snow White didn't mind; she was becoming accustomed to his broody quietness. Something about it was calming . . . perhaps because it was so familiar.

And besides, Snow White and Mouse had come up with

a new game—each guessing what the other was looking at. It was quite a bit similar to the game they had played earlier, but there were limited options in games that would keep them entertained as they walked.

The scenery had not changed much, the terrain remaining relatively even. Trees for miles and an ever-continuing path. And that was it. The Queen was clever in many ways, but oddly enough, she had not bothered to add much variance to the landscape.

Or perhaps she had, because Henry stumbled to a stop. His lunge forward was so abrupt and violent—as if he had just caught himself from falling over—that Snow White and Mouse immediately stopped their lively game.

"Don't come any closer," he said just as suddenly.

The two girls looked at each other. It was such a strange request that for a moment Snow White felt overwhelming concern and wanted to do nothing but the opposite of what Henry had asked. She looked at him—*really* looked, from the top of the back of his head down to his boots. His posture was stiff, and both feet were planted on the ground, spread in a firm base as if he was preparing himself for a fight. "Henry?"

"I can't move," he said, his voice uncertain, as if he didn't trust what he was saying himself. "My feet are stuck."

She and Mouse were no more than three feet behind him. Snow White studied the ground he was on. Nothing seemed out of the ordinary, but was anything really *ordinary* here? "What do you mean?"

"I can't lift my feet. As if my boots are stuck in something."

"Is it quicksand?" Mouse asked curiously. In true Mouse fashion, she sounded far too excited.

"I'm not sinking," he said, frustration coating his voice. "I just can't move."

He pulled on one leg, then the other, but it was no use. He couldn't pry them up from the ground even a little, and his feet weren't positioned well enough for him to keep his balance while pulling. After a few tries, he sighed, defeated. "Great. Just what we need right now."

"Hold on," said Snow White, assessing every inch of Henry again. She couldn't very well go to him and risk getting stuck herself. She looked around for a moment before settling on a tall blade of grass. Careful not to cut herself, she snapped the grass up and went back to where she had just been standing with Mouse. "Let's see where this sticky situation begins."

Snow White reached out to the ground with the long piece of jade, but it didn't seem to be affected by whatever was holding Henry. She crept a bit closer, keeping the blade of grass ahead of her to be sure she wouldn't get stuck—but even touching the spot where Henry's back foot was stuck resulted in nothing. She tapped the ground with the grass, then held it there. Nothing. It wouldn't stick.

There was a sharp sound, like the cracking of ice. It couldn't have been ice; it wasn't cold enough for that. But something solid, translucent, and pale blue crept up Henry's boot, stopping just below his ankle. Snow White wondered for a second what it reminded her of—rock candy, yes. How the crystals of delicious sugar formed and extended up the string.

Suddenly, Snow White's heart dropped into her feet. All she could think of was her dream of vicious hard gems climbing up her body, consuming her. This wasn't a world where something as innocent as rock candy would appear and they could just eat their way out of trouble. No, this was Diamant—the Queen's wicked creation. In no scenario were these climbing crystals going to taste delicious. And Snow White had a sinking feeling it wouldn't be quite as harmless, either.

"Henry," she said, forcing back panic, "can you get out of your boots?"

"Without falling over?" He hesitated, and she wished

he had gotten stuck facing her so she could see his expression. "I'll try."

He stabbed his sword into the ground—and Snow White saw the pale blue crystal retreat from the blade as he leaned on it with one hand to keep his balance. With the other he struggled with his boot. Snow White knew these boots; they were a bit higher up the calf than most boots and normally fit so perfectly that one had to drag them off with both hands. And poor Henry—as much as he tried, his foot wasn't budging. And then he had to snatch his hand away to keep the gems from biting his fingers as they crawled up to his ankle.

"Okay," he said, his voice more distressed than she had ever heard it before, "this hurts now. It's really pressing in."

"What's happening to Henry?" Mouse asked, standing at a safe distance.

Henry yanked up his sword and used the flat end to try to break up the climbing gemstones. It worked to a point; clearly the gems must have been weaker than diamonds. And strangely enough, the gems he broke didn't grow back in that particular place. But he wasn't at the right angle to hit hard enough without potentially cutting himself. Even though she could only see Henry's back, Snow White could tell he was wincing.

"Don't hurt yourself, Henry," she said.

"It hurts enough without me hitting it," he snapped.

Knowing he was in pain upset her, but she couldn't lose her nerve now. "Don't panic."

"Is he turning into a creature like one of the gem wolves?" asked Mouse.

Snow White took a deep breath, remembering Jonathan's fate in her dream, and for a moment, she thought *she* might panic. But she wasn't helpless. She could do something about it. She *had* to. "Not if I have anything to say about it."

She needed to find a way to get to Henry to help, but there was no walking over there—or was there?

The grass. It had not been affected by whatever this trap was. Perhaps the gemstones of Diamant couldn't affect their fellow gemstones.

"Henry," she said, "hand me your sword."

"I thought you didn't like swords."

She huffed. "This really isn't the time."

Snow White knew he would have been side-eyeing her if he could have safely turned around. But he handed his sword back to her anyway, with the hilt facing her. It was heavier than she had thought it would be, but that made it all the more useful for what she needed it to do.

It was time for a little trimming.

She went to the edge of the path and sliced at the grass. The sword was so weighty and sharp that she chopped the grass down easily. She chopped and sliced until her arms were burning from the effort of swinging his sword.

"Stardrop," said Henry nervously, "whatever you're doing over there, *hurry*."

She took his desperation to heart. One more swing was enough. She scooped up an armful of jade, but when she turned around, she nearly dropped it again. Henry's legs were enveloped practically to the tops of his boots.

There was no way she was going to let her nightmare come true.

She laid some of the grass out in front of her, creating a pathway—well, the start of one. Stepping onto it was nerve-racking, but she sighed in relief when she saw her theory had been right: the gems were unaffected by each other. So she continued laying the path to get to Henry, stepping on the grass as she went, until she was in front of him. She had to work quickly, stuffing grass along the tops of Henry's boots in hopes that the gems wouldn't grow over the grass and it would give her time to figure out how to get Henry out.

She lifted his sword, then paused. No. It was too sharp and heavy. She could easily hurt him if she struck the creeping gems too hard or in the wrong way. This was a delicate process, with Henry's legs hanging in the balance.

But she had to remember that she had been the one to touch the map. The magic in the map and the trials they were facing were all catered to her now. That meant everything here would be something she could complete on her own. But it also meant everything would be solved *her* way, not with brute strength like Henry would use.

She had to think quickly through her other options.

Well, what did she know about the crystal? It stayed away from the other gems, for one thing. That meant . . .

"Henry," she said, "I'm going to pry your feet up. When I do, try to step onto the grass I've laid out."

Henry was grimacing, uncomfortable. But he nodded, because what other choice did he have? It was that or be eaten alive by a creeping crystal.

Henry's sword was much easier to handle when all the weight was pointed downward. Carefully, Snow White poked Henry's sword at the base of his boot, prying the edge beneath it. It came up easier than she had thought it would, and maybe Henry wasn't ready for it to happen so quickly, because the sudden loosening made him lose his balance, with the heaviness of the crystal encasing the lower half of his leg sending him flailing to catch himself. The action made Mouse scream.

When Henry's foot came down, it missed the grass completely. He was stuck again, but at least he hadn't fallen over. They were back where they had started, only this time, Snow White knew what to do—and what *not* to do.

She would have to help direct his heavy crystal-encased feet to safety.

"This is stressful!" cried Mouse. She covered her eyes and turned around so she wouldn't have to see whatever horrible thing happened next.

Snow White and Henry looked at each other. They didn't need to hear Mouse say that to know it was true. If Henry lost his balance the wrong way when Snow White pried him loose, and he fell into the crystal . . . She didn't even want to think about it.

"Okay," she said, attempting to steady her breathing. "Try to remain calm, Henry. The grass is right beside you. All you have to do is take a small step to the side."

"My legs are so heavy," he said. He was panting, his face strained from his last effort to move his leg and, to Snow White's dismay, clearly from pain. "I don't know if I can."

"You can do it, Henry. You have to."

Again he nodded. Snow White wanted to get him out as quickly as possible, but she couldn't rush the process.

She had the easy part. He was the one who had to steer that heavy leg while in discomfort and pain.

But when she pried his boot free, he did his very best to move it while she used the flat edge of the sword to direct his foot sideways. They both let out a breath of relief as his foot landed on the grass.

"That's one leg on safe ground," said Snow White, trying to sound encouraging. "Now we just have to clear the other, and you can walk out of here. And then you'll get to sit. Won't that be nice?"

Snow White couldn't tell if Henry was glaring at her or was just in pain. Either way, he didn't see the bright side to the event whatsoever. "And then? I'll still have massive chunks of crystal on my legs."

"We will deal with that when we get there," said Snow White. "Are you ready?"

Henry took a deep breath. "Ready."

She pried his front foot free, and he did his best to step where she guided him. And that was it. Both feet were planted on the safe grass.

When Henry tried to take a step with his heavy foot, Snow White ran to him, then dropped his sword without a thought as she got behind him and caught him around the waist.

"Let go," Henry said quickly. "I feel like I'm going to fall on you."

"I've got you, Henry," she insisted. When she was sure Henry had regained his balance, she stood in front of him, facing their path to freedom. "Here, hold on to my shoulders to keep your balance. And take it slow."

Snow White held her shoulders firm as Henry rested his hands on them. She took slow steps forward, allowing Henry to catch up one heavy step at a time. The pressure and unevenness of his hands fluctuated as he kept himself balanced with each movement. Finally, Henry took a final step onto solid ground, and Mouse cheered.

When Henry was certain he wasn't going to stick to crystalized ground again, he sat down without much help, though with lots of wincing. "I can't move my feet at all," he said.

"What does it feel like?" Mouse asked, staring at his legs in awe.

"Like two boa constrictors with dull thorns attached to their stomachs trying to crush my legs to dust," he said, thoroughly unamused. "Thanks for asking."

"Here, Mouse." Snow White handed the little girl a blade of grass. "You take his left leg. I'll do his right. Just pry up the crystal with the tip of the jade, and it should come away."

Mouse squinted at her work, poking the blade beneath the crystal near the top of Henry's boot. Her eyes shone as a bit of it came away. "Oooooh! That's a cool trick."

"Could you work a little more," Henry grumbled, "and enjoy it a little less?"

"Be patient," said Snow White. "There's only so much these thin blades of grass can do at one time."

"And by the way," he said, irritated, "you didn't have to drop my sword. Do you know how long it took me to make that without the proper tools?"

"It was either drop the sword or let you fall and hurt yourself."

"Well, this already hurts," he snapped. "So I pick saving the sword next time."

"Stop being so mean to Snow White!" Mouse snapped back. "She saved you from becoming a gemstone statue."

Henry couldn't argue with that, so he made a grumbling sound of discontent but said nothing else. Snow White and Mouse worked—well, Snow White did, but Mouse got frustrated and bored with the task before long—until every last piece of gemstone had been stripped from Henry's boots.

When she was done, Henry fell backward to lie down. He closed his eyes, cringing as he took deep breaths. He was free from that horrible trap, but the aftermath didn't seem any easier.

"What can I do, Henry?" Snow White asked.

"Nothing," he groused. "The pain isn't sharp anymore. I'm certain my legs are just bruised."

His wince when trying to shift them implied more than bruises were hindering him.

"Perhaps we should give them a little break, then," said Snow White, reaching for one of his boots. "So nothing is pressing against them."

"No," he said, "don't take them off. They won't go on again comfortably in this state, and we have to get moving soon."

"Give yourself a few minutes, at least."

"We have a lot of ground to cover before it gets dark. We've lost enough time as it is."

Snow White laid her hands against Henry's chest, gently guiding him back down as he tried to sit up. "Ten minutes' delay won't make any difference. Just rest."

Henry sighed but didn't try to get up again. "Can I have my sword back?"

Snow White sighed right back but dragged it up from the ground to hand it to him. He stayed on his back, holding it up to examine it for any damages.

"Will Henry be able to travel now?" Mouse asked. "With all the running we've been having to do, maybe he should go back to town."

"And leave you two in the wilderness alone?" said Henry, raising a brow. "Thanks for the laugh."

Mouse scowled, planting her hands on her hips. "You're going to slow us down with your two crystal-eaten legs."

"Says the child who takes more breaks than an infant."

"Well, at least I won't have to *crawl* like an infant for the rest of the journey!" Mouse stuck her tongue out at him, finishing the argument.

"There's no need for all this fighting, you two," said Snow White. "Henry, are you sure there's nothing we can do? If there are Forgetting Stones, there must be some sort of healing stone here, too, right?"

"I've never heard of something like that," said Mouse with a shrug. "And anyway, when we stay inside the walls, no one gets hurt. We've never had to deal with any of this!"

"But there's good magic here," said Snow White, "along with the evil. Anything wicked the gems here can do, there must be something that can counterbalance it."

"There is something," Henry said, and his two companions turned to look at him. He cringed. "Never mind. It's impossible to find."

"If it will help you," said Snow White, "then it's more than worth it."

He sighed, leaning up on his elbows. "Wishing Grain." At his words Mouse blew raspberries, and he rolled his eyes before continuing. "I've seen them used before. The legend is when the Queen learned of the Ruby Heart, she tried to destroy it, but all she managed to do was chip away pieces of it. Those pieces became scattered, but they're supposed to have some of the wish-granting abilities of the Ruby Heart. I saw one grain heal a man's broken arm."

"Well, it's settled, then. We'll find Wishing Grain," said Snow White.

"It's too dangerous," Henry groaned.

"Your being hurt is a danger. We can't travel with you in this condition. Let me go and find the one thing that can help you."

Henry sighed, defeated. "Where there are crows, there's usually Wishing Grain. They like to hoard it."

"They like to *collect* and bestow *gifts*," Snow White said, correcting him. She grinned. "This shouldn't take long. I'm very familiar with how to find crows."

"Friends of yours?" he asked.

"Just stay here and rest. Oh, and I'll need your sword."

"You refused a sword when I offered it to you, and now

this will make the second time you're using mine. Make up your mind, will you?"

"Your sword, please?" She held out her hand to Henry until he reluctantly handed his sword to her. "I'll be back soon."

"I'm coming, too!" Mouse said, and hopped over to stand beside Snow White.

"Perfect," said Snow White, hugging her around the shoulders. "It takes two to steal from crows effectively. But first"—she stabbed the blade of the sword into the ground and then looked up into the trees—"we have to find out where these birds live."

She set to climbing the nearest tree, with Mouse, not wanting to miss a single moment, right behind her. But gemstone trees were significantly smoother than normal ones back home, which had delightful bark to grip on to. Fortunately, the branches were close enough together that Snow White could climb them like an uneven ladder, one to the next. Mouse bypassed Snow White by climbing on the opposite side of the tree, then sat at the top and waited, kicking her feet. The branches were uncomfortably narrow closer to the top, and part of Snow White doubted that they could hold both her and Mouse. But climbing the tree was only step one—the easiest step, to be honest. If Snow White couldn't get through this, there was no hope of stealing from crows.

But there was no sense in going into it with any doubts, so she let them fade to the back of her mind as she reached the top.

The sun was far brighter up there, with the leaves reflecting it forcefully. For a moment, Snow White had a hard time finding what she was looking for. She knew that if there were crows to be found, they would be made of some sort of gemstone, too, and might reflect the light just as brightly as the emerald leaves.

But lo and behold, she spotted bird-shaped creatures about a mile away, roosting at the top of a slightly taller tree than the one she and Mouse had climbed. The blinding light made it difficult to determine their coloring, but Snow White was confident they were similar to crows back in her world.

This was going to be over with more quickly than she had thought.

"We'll be back," Snow White called to Henry when she and Mouse had made it to the bottom. She rested the flat of his blade against her shoulder, and Henry watched them go with a skeptical look on his face.

They walked casually—or at least not at the intense pace

Henry loved to make them keep up, with his long strides and no-nonsense approach to never losing the sunlight. They could not risk startling the crows before the time was right. If the creatures became territorial and began defending their home, there was no real hope of retrieving what they had come for.

And if the crows were anything like the wolves there, Snow White and Mouse would have to be extra careful.

"I just thought of something," said Mouse, picking up a loose stick on the ground. "What if we run into wolves again?"

"We know how to tame them now," Snow White said simply.

"Oh, right." They walked in silence—for less than a second, seeing as Mouse was there. "What if one goes after Henry?"

"He'll be just fine, Mouse. Honestly, as much as I hate to see him in pain, I'm glad he's resting for once."

"Yeah, me too. He walks too fast for me." Mouse paused. "But how do you know those are crows? What if they're some other bird? What if we're walking all this way for nothing?"

"Crows like to have family gatherings at the tops of

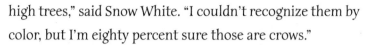

high trees," said Snow White. "I couldn't recognize them by color, but I'm eighty percent sure those are crows."

"What if we get there and the twenty percent of you that's *not* sure it's crows is right?"

"Well, now you just sound like Henry."

"Ew!" Mouse hung her tongue out of her mouth, then wiped it with her hands to emphasize how incredibly little she cared for that comparison. "I don't want to be Henry."

Snow White ruffled the giggling girl's hair. "Then no negativity allowed."

But they hadn't gone ten more steps before the little girl blurted, "I think we should just send him home," as if she'd been holding it in.

"He can't walk home right now any more than he can continue the journey. The Wishing Grain will make everything right."

"But he's been on a lot of journeys to find the Ruby Heart and has failed every time. He's bad luck or something."

Snow White frowned but continued walking quickly. "Stop that now, Mouse. He is not bad luck."

"Either he's bad luck or there's no Ruby Heart."

"Mouse," Snow White said firmly. "Don't say such things."

He might have been grumpy, but that did not make him a bringer of misfortune.

"We all left town together," said Snow White, "and that's how we'll return." She adjusted the sword on her shoulder and continued walking.

Mouse shuffled behind her but eventually forgot her pouting and ran ahead, doing figure eights around trees.

When they were a quarter of a mile away, Snow White stopped, pulling Mouse behind a tree. "Okay, Mouse, here's the plan. You'll climb up this tree and use Henry's sword to reflect the sun and distract them. Then, when you have them flying in your direction, I'll sneak into their secret hollow."

"What secret hollow?" Mouse asked, scrunching her nose.

"Don't you know? All crows have a secret hollow." Snow White whispered like it was a secret.

She watched wonder light up in Mouse's eyes as Mouse asked, "Where?"

"I'm not sure." Snow White hesitated. "But I am sure it won't be difficult to find."

"But wait a second," Mouse said, worry returning to her face. "What if when I'm distracting the crows, they try to claw my eyes out?"

"You wanted to come along, so you'll have to be brave and do your part. Besides, you'll have the sword to defend yourself."

Mouse brightened, as if she'd never considered that. "Oh, yeah."

"Okay, are you ready?"

"Ready." Mouse grinned.

Snow White rushed off toward the tree that housed the crows, then took a deep breath before climbing it. She moved carefully, so as not to cause a disturbance. She couldn't very well have them focused on her when she was trying to steal from them. She gripped the tree tightly as it shook, and when she looked up, most of the crows had flown off. Their plan was working, even if Snow White couldn't see the glint from Henry's sword in Mouse's hands from where she hid among the branches.

But perhaps she had celebrated too soon, because as Mouse had made her admit, she had no idea where the crows kept their treasure hollow. She'd have to look quickly or else risk losing all the time Mouse was buying for her. With the crows gone and cawing in the distance, she heard the tiny little chirps of baby chicks.

That was a start.

A few feet above her sat a nest, and when Snow White

climbed high enough to peek inside she saw it housed five tiny chicks. For a moment Snow White thought that she had been mistaken, that they weren't crows after all. They were golden orange, like a hot sunset, and slightly transparent, instead of black, as crows should be. But she suddenly realized it was because they were made of amber. Little gnats and spiders were stuck inside their bodies, forever preserved. It was a bit unsettling, as cute as the chicks themselves were, so she turned her focus to the trunk of the tree, where there was a small hole. Snow White let out a breath in relief and, careful not to disturb the nest, peeked inside. Sure enough, this was the crows' treasure hollow. There were gems of all kinds inside, but also knives and jewelry—and small crimson pebbles.

This had to be the Wishing Grain. The pieces were uneven and not uniform in shape—a clear sign that they had indeed been broken from a larger source. They were small, technically pebbles but some of them resembled grains of rice. And they were rubies to be sure—well, not to be *sure*, as there were other red gemstones that were possibilities. But when the other facts were placed beside the color, Snow White was positive this was the Wishing Grain.

And they glowed and glistened enough that they could have been nothing but magical.

The crow chicks began to chirp as if they were hungry. The last thing she needed was for the parents to hear them and fly back to see what was wrong. *Don't dawdle, Snow White.* Carefully, she reached her hand into the hole and picked up all the pieces she could find. The more she collected, the more the little chicks screeched, as if they were the security guards of all the crows' treasures.

"Oh, no, little ones, don't cry," she cooed, but as their volume increased, her heart panicked. "Please stop crying. . . ."

She tucked the Wishing Grain deep into the pocket of her skirt.

And the chicks went berserk.

"Oh no, oh no, oh no . . ." Snow White looked up quickly, and through the leaves and branches she could see the forms of crows returning.

The screeching had caught the attention the chicks had been looking for—and the attention Snow White wanted nothing to do with.

By the time Snow White had made it to the ground, a handful of them had begun to swoop, their amber bodies easy enough to see while at the same time impossible to track. She'd forgotten—*again*—that the animals were not like the ones at home. Or perhaps she had hoped that because the person who had made the animals didn't know much about the creatures, they were just generalized versions: wolves were predators in real life, so here that was all they were. Crows were curious, so here they were nothing else but.

But Snow White had miscalculated. The Queen was evil, and nothing here meant them any good, regardless of the way animals behaved in real life.

"Mouse!" she called as she ran, her arms covering her head to protect her from the constant swooping from all directions. She was thankful she had grabbed extra Wishing Grain; Henry had mentioned that just one could heal a broken arm; she hoped that was all he needed now. She threw a couple, and a few of her pursuers took the bait and flew off to retrieve them. But as she was distracted, a large crow swooped and knocked her off-balance. She fell to her hands and knees, and her attempt to stand again was interrupted by a massive crow landing in front of her.

It squawked a warning, a dangerous sound that was less crow-like and more monstrous.

Snow White was absolutely positive she wanted nothing more to do with these crows.

She fished another Wishing Grain from her pocket, and

fortunately, when she threw it, it distracted the crow long enough for her to get to her feet and run. She saw Mouse ahead, dragging Henry's sword behind her, with the crows all over it, trying to pick up the heavy thing and take it to their treasure hollow.

"Snow White!" Mouse cried, hanging her head back in despair. "They won't go away!"

Snow White caught up to Mouse and took the sword from her. "Shoo!" she shouted, and Mouse copied her, shouting "Shoo, birds!" over and over without doing much else. Snow White picked up the sword—holding it low, only at knee level, since the multitude of amber birds perched and pulling on it weighed it down significantly—and tapped it against the closest tree. As the crows began flying off, the blade became lighter, until Snow White could slam it into the tree, making all the creatures scatter with angry squawks.

Snow White took all but one Wishing Grain from her pocket and threw it away from her, sending a majority of the crows flying toward it. "Run, Mouse!" she shouted, and the two of them took off running as fast as they could.

The crows either had lost interest or were sufficiently convinced that their territory had been secured and their chicks were safe, because after a bit of sprinting, Snow White and Mouse could finally slow down to a walk. As they caught their breath, the two of them looked at each other . . . and broke into laughter.

"That was *fun!*" said Mouse.

"It was certainly an adventure." It was a bit fun, admittedly—though more *after* the fact than during, in Snow White's opinion. The whole idea of it—being chased by crows—was rather ridiculous. Of course, by the Queen's orders, Snow White had been chased by armed soldiers only a little while before she bit the apple in the real world, so comparatively, crows were most definitely a lot more fun.

"Let's get this to Henry," Snow White said, retrieving the last Wishing Grain from her pocket, "and be on our way."

Henry was still where they had left him, fortunately in one piece, his hands behind his head as he lay on his back. But at Mouse's exclamation of "We got it!" he sat up and looked over his shoulder.

"You what?" he said, pure disbelief in his voice.

Snow White took his hand, holding it palm up so she could place the Wishing Grain in it.

Henry gaped. "Where did you find it?"

"I told you I knew where to find crows," said Snow White. She patted his shoulder. For a moment Henry was at a loss for words; he certainly tried, opening his mouth a few times before closing it again. Finally, he simply sighed and closed his eyes. And he must have wished, because Snow White watched as the grain crumbled to the finest dust in his palm. He brushed off his hands and carefully got to his feet.

"Did it work?" Snow White asked.

"It worked." Henry threw his pack over his shoulder as if nothing had been wrong a moment earlier. "Let's get moving."

Relief washed over her. "Good. But if I see you wincing, we're going to immediately stop to rest."

"Then I shall endeavor to be stoic."

Snow White laughed at how seriously he had said it. "You can't hide from me, Henry. I will be watching you like a hawk." To prove it, she circled him, observing his stance.

The smallest grin broke through Henry's mask of grouchiness, but he quickly went about chopping down grass before she could draw attention to it. And then she and Mouse helped him spread the grass over the spot where he had gotten stuck, using the blades to cross to safe ground.

Once they were across, Henry clapped his hands. "It

appears the Queen has been more creative with her traps than anticipated."

"All the more reason to disappoint her," Snow White said, smiling.

Her brief moment of hope was interrupted by the cawing of crows. They all looked to see that the murder was heading toward them—not the full family Snow White and Mouse had fought off, but enough of them to cause a lot more trouble than Snow White would like.

Although, *no* trouble would be preferable.

"Ah, your friends have returned," said Henry, giving Snow White a pointed look.

"Why did we have to steal their things?" lamented Mouse. "Now they're back to eat us!"

Snow White swallowed. Mouse was right: they didn't seem happy to have discovered what was missing. Snow White grabbed Henry's arm. "We should go."

"You mean you don't want to say hello?" Henry asked sarcastically as Snow White dragged him away. He looked over his shoulder, his expression becoming more serious. "We'll lose them across the river. The other side is where their territory ends. They won't bother to pursue us farther."

But if they wanted to lose them at all, there was no time to be careful and avoid any discoloration on the path that meant another crystal trap. They just had to hope they wouldn't run into any of that. They just needed to run.

Snow White held out her hands, accepted the pack from Henry, and put it on her back. Henry bent down, helping Mouse climb onto his back, holding on to her legs while she wrapped her arms around his neck. And they took off running.

Those crows intended to take revenge and take it swiftly.

"They're getting closer!" Mouse cried, and Snow White didn't want to look again but heard the screeching becoming ever louder. They were monsters, plain and simple, as much as the Queen had designed them to look like crows. And maybe there were thorns in their backs causing them to act this way, like there had been with the wolves. But the crows didn't seem like they were going to give the three of them time to soothe them and find out.

"The river is just ahead," shouted Henry.

And it was, fortunately, just beyond the curve of the path. They skidded to a stop at the river. It was moving at a casual pace, but moving nonetheless, and they were unable to tell if it was flowing too quickly for them to safely swim across. Not to mention the surface was not clear, murky from troubled dirt on the riverbed, so it was impossible to

tell how deep it was. But again, the details were not important. Surviving was.

Henry tried to put Mouse down, but she clung to him,
nearly choking him with her arms around his neck.

"I can't swim," she said, clinging to him for dear life.

"I'm going to carry you, you silly girl," Henry said impa-
tiently. "Now let go."

"I don't want to get wet."

"Black cauldrons," he swore. "Then get killed by the
crows. We don't have time for this."

The little girl howled and began weeping, and Henry,
thoroughly unamused, winced from the piercing volume
near his ear.

"You're scaring her, Henry," Snow White said, giving
him a disapproving look. She glanced behind them, at the
crows drawing nearer, far too close for comfort. "You're
sure we just need to cross the river?"

"It shouldn't be too far from here. We're almost there,"
Henry said quickly, finally prying the crying girl's fingers
off and setting her on the ground. "Can you swim in that
dress?"

"I'll have to," Snow White said. It would get heavy, but
that didn't matter at the moment.

Henry took the pack from her and put it on his back

before getting into the water. "Freezing," he muttered, cringing in reaction to the river's temperature, but he didn't stop. So far the water was only up to his waist as he stood. "On my shoulders," he said, turning around.

Mouse clung to Snow White, but she coaxed the girl forward with soft words and a gentle push—and got her to sit on Henry's shoulders just as a crow swooped down at Snow White's head.

"Get in," said Henry. "I have my sword. Mouse and I will catch up."

"You'll never even make it to the middle."

"Get in the water," he said, his concern coming out as anger. "Are you out of your mind?" But he started walking along the river's floor, his body traveling deeper under the surface the farther in he went.

Maybe she was out of her mind; after all, Henry had his sword, and she had nothing but her arms to defend herself. But she wanted to give them a moment and a head start. She would be swimming and get to the other side faster than they would walking.

So she yelled and waved her hands at the crows that swooped until her friends were a quarter of the way across the river. And then she dived into the river and swam for her life.

The current wasn't strong at all, and if anything, it helped her a little toward the opposite shore, even if it did send her at a bit of an angle. It was only when she reached the other side that a problem presented itself: her dress had not weighed her down much while she swam, but she felt fifty pounds heavier in all that soaked fabric as she tried to pull herself onto shore.

Mouse screamed in distress, and when Snow White looked up, she saw three crows swooping at the girl's head. She and Henry weren't at the halfway point yet; the crows and Mouse's frantic screams were slowing Henry's progress. Snow White threw herself into action, digging her nails into the dirt to grip it and dragging her weighed-down body onto the bank. Water poured from her dress, and it was hard to get up, but her friends needed her. She reached up to the nearest tree and grabbed some leaves. She didn't think about it too much—if at all, lest she doubt her aim—and threw a stone in the direction of the crows. It didn't hit any of them, but it was enough to make one decide that these humans were not worth its time. That left only two more.

She threw another one, and it narrowly missed Mouse's head. It scared the crows for a moment, but it did not deter them for long.

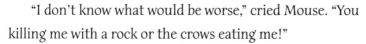

"I don't know what would be worse," cried Mouse. "You killing me with a rock or the crows eating me!"

"Mouse," Snow White called, "duck!"

Still screaming, the little girl tucked her head and covered it with her arms while Henry shouted, "For the love of everything, stop screaming!"

"Okay, rock," Snow White whispered, "don't hit my friends."

She continued her volley of stones, which never hit a single bird but disturbed their flight patterns and kept them away from Mouse and Henry. And soon it became enough of a nuisance to convince the remaining crows to leave.

Snow White sighed in relief. With the threat of attacking crows gone, she began squeezing out the skirt of her dress. With the amount of water pouring onto the ground, she could have filled a bathtub.

Henry and Mouse finally made it to where Snow White was waiting for them, and Mouse reached up to Snow White, who helped her off Henry's shoulders and set her on the riverbank. Mouse lay on her back, her mouth trembling with emotion. Snow White couldn't blame her. Somehow that crow attack had been far more traumatic than their first encounter.

"My shoes are all wet," the little girl whimpered.

Snow White was reminded then that Mouse was still a child, and perhaps Henry had been right about who belonged on quests. "We're all wet together, Mouse," Snow White said sweetly. "It's okay. The sun will help us dry off."

"But it's uncomfortable," she said, and fell into tears again.

Snow White pulled the little girl into a hug. She locked eyes with Henry and saw the annoyance in his expression.

Snow White sighed. "Have some compassion, Henry. She's just a little girl."

Henry wrung out his shirt, scowling at the amount of water that rained down onto his boots. "We don't have time to stop every time Mouse is inconvenienced."

"We just stopped for you, remember!" Mouse shouted, her little voice sounding heartbroken.

"I was injured. Your shoes are wet. There's a difference." He began to walk away, but Snow White stopped him with a stern expression, and he at least had the decency to look slightly ashamed of himself as he added, "I know we're all tired, but we have a lot of ground to cover before sundown."

He continued walking.

She shook her head after him and knelt down beside Mouse. "What do you want to do, Mouse? Do you maybe want to take them off? I can hold them for you until they dry."

Mouse stopped crying and blinked away the remainder of her tears, sniffling a little. "Okay," she said. She pulled her shoes off and handed them to Snow White before leaping to her feet with a renewed energy and skipping off to catch up with Henry. "Let's go, Snow White! Hurry up!"

Snow White grinned—granted in a slightly confused manner. Mouse certainly was a fan of the dramatic. Snow White tied the little girl's laces together and hung the shoes around her neck before rushing to catch up with her companions.

The day seemed to be endless. They continued following the path on the map, but on the opposite side of the river. Snow White and Henry walked beside each other while Mouse adventured ahead in their view, running and climbing trees and trying to catch high-springing crickets. Her feet didn't seem to hurt even the slightest bit pounding against all the hard gems, and she didn't seem concerned about leading the pack at all, considering that Henry had just had to be rescued from a trap and they had almost been murdered by, well, a murder. But maybe that was healthy. One couldn't go through life fearing what-ifs.

"Henry," Snow White said after a while of enjoying the journey in silence, "can I ask you something?"

"I think we both know you're just going to ask anyway no matter my response."

"How can you be . . . almost whimsical when it comes to the magic of the map, but then be such a gloomy realist when it comes to the rest of the world?"

"Whimsical?" He looked a bit surprised. "That is not a word I thought would ever be associated with me."

"It's not like being whimsical is a bad thing."

"The map works," he said, clearly annoyed that he and the word *whimsical* were being used in relation to each other. "It's the only magic I trust around here."

"Why? If this is a world created by the Queen, how can you trust anything made here?"

"I don't know, to be honest. I don't know who made it. It was found in a hollow of one of the trees when the town was first being built. But it's our only hope. We have to trust *something*."

"We can trust each other," said Snow White.

He gave her a skeptical look, but one that bordered on teasing. "I don't know. Trusting you gets us chased by falling emeralds."

"And trusting *you* gets us nearly eaten by wolves."

Snow White cracked a smile before Henry, who rubbed his face to hide his.

Mouse laughed loudly as she spun enough to make herself dizzy. She staggered around for a bit, giggling, until she fell over.

"She's been here so long," Snow White said with fondness and admiration in her voice, "and is still so joyful. It's beautiful to see."

"She's accepted her fate," said Henry, his voice taking on a serious tone.

"Perhaps not. Or else why would she come with us? She must believe we can find the way home."

"She's just bored."

Snow White looked up at him, searching his expression. "You don't seem to think very much of her."

Henry was quiet for a moment. "She just takes all of this so lightly."

"I think that's okay. I suppose she considers Diamant her home now. Everyone copes with things differently."

Henry looked at her quickly, pausing his gait for a moment before scowling and continuing on.

Snow White pursed her lips at his reaction. She couldn't understand why the two of them always butted heads. "Do you two have some sort of . . . discord between you?"

Henry scoffed. "I'm a disturber of the peace according to half the town, Mouse included. Or I was when I used to encourage people to go with me to find the Ruby Heart." He hesitated for a moment, then shrugged. "But I don't do that anymore, so . . ."

"That's awful."

"Now you're probably the one they whisper about."

"Me?" Snow White gaped.

"You've disturbed their peace." Henry shrugged again, this time with a small grin. "On the upside, you're not really one of us until you've had your turn as the target of vicious gossip. So I suppose I can now truly welcome you to Diamant."

"Well, things will be different when we bring the Ruby Heart back," Snow White said with a shrug.

"*If* we bring it back."

"*When.*" Snow White gave him a pointed look.

Henry shook his head. "Your unrealistic expectations are just . . . frustrating. Yes, we'll go with 'frustrating.' It's the politest option."

"Come now, Henry, don't act like you don't like me, either."

His only response was a grumble.

"What *do* you like?" Snow White demanded good-naturedly. "Do you actually like anything?"

"Do I *like* anything?" Henry raised a brow.

"What are your hobbies, your dreams? What makes you happy?"

Henry seemed to scowl a little less, and that was all Snow White had wanted—to break through his wall, if only a bit. "I have to tell you, you're a little too nosy for my liking right now."

"I know what you like to do," Snow White said, giving him a sly look. "Bladesmithing."

"That's my vocation. It just happens to be useful here." He paused, then sighed. "I mean, I do enjoy it—"

"Aha!" Snow White poked him in the arm, and she could tell he was trying not to laugh. "I knew it."

"I don't think a skill counts as a hobby if you need it to survive."

"All right, then." Snow White tapped her chin, studying him. "If bladesmithing can't count as your hobby, then it must be—"

"Why don't we talk about *your* hobbies?" he cut in. "It's only fair."

"My hobbies?" Snow White paused a moment to think.

Half of her childhood, she had not been allowed to have much fun—because the Queen had not thought very highly of happiness and fun. She had had her wishing well to visit but not many activities.

Henry chuckled, waking her from her thoughts. "Stardrop, are you at a loss for words? It's a miracle."

"Oh, hush, Henry."

"We should document this moment."

"Well, if you must know, I love dancing."

Henry scoffed. "Isn't that a requirement for princesses?"

"You really shouldn't make assumptions." Snow White smiled. "Besides, being required to do something is different from loving to do it."

"Fair enough."

"But either way," she said, grinning, "you can't deny that I'm great at it."

"Great at what?"

Snow White gaped and then poked him in the arm. "Dancing, you silly goose."

Henry was smiling, unable to hide it anymore. "You're passable at best."

Snow White stepped in front of Henry, halting him in his tracks. "Excuse *me*, sir. Is that a challenge?"

Henry's expression dropped. "Absolutely not."

"We both know you enjoy dancing as much as I do." Snow White giggled, hooking her arm through his as they continued on to catch up with Mouse. "We had a wonderful time last night, didn't we?"

"Yeah," Henry murmured in a tone that expressed he was unwilling to admit he was capable of having fun.

"But what I would like to know is why it takes the use of a Forgetting Stone for you to allow yourself to experience joy."

Henry's steps faltered, and he escaped from her grasp. "I'd rather not talk about it."

"But you were so different last night. You seemed so happy. So free."

"Let's just focus on getting where we're going without incident," he said. "Who knows what other traps we'll run into—"

"Henry." Snow White rushed to step in front of him. She held up her hands to halt him. "Henry, please. What was it last night that you wished to forget? If you tell me, maybe I can help you."

He shook his head, clearly unable to look at her when he said, "It's not important."

"It must cause you a great amount of pain if you resorted to magic to forget it."

Henry paused as if measuring her words. But still he refused to look at her. "It feels too ridiculous to admit it out loud. You'll laugh at me."

"Of course I won't," Snow White said gently.

Henry was silent for a moment, chewing on the inside of his cheek. Snow White gave him the time he needed, despite Mouse's adventuring farther and farther ahead of them.

Finally, Henry released the words "I want to go home" all in one breath, as if he couldn't have done it otherwise. "Even if I have no home to go back to."

Snow White sucked in a breath. Those words, those feelings, weren't what she had expected from him. From the one who had saved her from the wolves the previous day, who seemed so well-adjusted to life there. Henry... wanted to go home.

Well, they had that in common.

More than ever, she wanted to find the Ruby Heart. Her own heart needed her to, and not just for her kingdom and her friends in the real world, not just for the crying woman she'd met the night before.

Her friend—they were friends, weren't they?—was in need.

Snow White reached out to him, touching his arm gently to comfort him. "Oh, Henry—"

"Hey, slowpokes!" shouted Mouse. "Catch up!"

Snow White and Henry looked at each other, words hanging between them.

"I wanted to forget the feeling," Henry said finally. "And I want to forget this conversation. Don't ask me again."

"I won't bring it up if that's what you want," said Snow White. "But—"

"Let's leave it there, shall we?" Henry adjusted his pack on his shoulder. "We have a lot of ground to cover," he murmured, and pressed on.

Henry didn't speak much to either Snow White or Mouse for the rest of the day—which would have seemed normal if Snow White hadn't been certain that she'd just felt a spark of friendship between them before she had gone and asked such a personal question. Henry kept them walking at a brisk pace, and Snow White was sure it was so that her legs couldn't keep up with his, so that she couldn't bring up the subject again of what he'd wished to forget.

Perhaps he didn't realize that he had said something lovely and not at all awful. That missing his home was nothing to be ashamed of. As it stood, after an hour of his silence, every time Snow White tried to say something to him, he gave her a very general answer or simply continued on as if he had not heard her. Better than the first hour, but still rather petty, and Snow White was beginning to wonder if there was maybe more to his silence than he was letting on.

The sinking sun gave them no choice but to stop, and Henry set up camp—"camp" being a pile of coals out in the open for them to sleep around. It was chilly.

After such a long, eventful day of travel, it seemed impossible that this was only their first night sleeping outside the town. Snow White couldn't help looking at the big wide sky, stars speckling it with magic.

They settled down quickly and gratefully, thoroughly exhausted from the intense adventures they'd had that day—all except Mouse, it seemed, as she lay on her back and kicked her legs in the air.

"Let's look for shooting stars," she said, full of energy and excitement, "so we can make wishes."

"Shooting stars are very rare, Mouse," said Snow White, lying on her stomach and using her crossed forearms as a pillow. "But you can make wishes upon regular stars."

"Oooh!" Mouse rubbed her hands together. "I'm going to wish on a big one." She scanned the sky for a moment. "Whoa . . . which star is that?" she asked, pointing up. "What's that one called?"

"How are either of us supposed to know which of the

billions of stars you're pointing to?" Henry mumbled rhetorically. He lit the pile of coals laid out at the center of the three of them.

Snow White shook her head at him, then rolled onto her back to look at the sky, too. "Which star, Mouse?"

"That big, bright one. Near the moon."

"Oh. Well." She looked at it for a moment. How strange—but wonderful—that this unreal world contained something as familiar as stars. "We could always make up a name for it."

"Ooh, yes!" Mouse thought for a moment, scrunching up her nose. "Lightning Bug. Bug for short."

"How wonderfully charming. Hello up there, Bug!"

"Let's wish on it, Snow White," Mouse said, and closed her eyes tight. "Grant my wish, Lightning Bug. Don't let me down!"

Snow White smiled and closed her eyes. Perhaps she could wish on these stars. Perhaps she could wish for home.

"What did you wish for?" Mouse asked.

Snow White giggled at the little girl's enthusiasm. "You can't tell anyone your wish, or else your dream won't come true. When it comes true, I'll let you know."

"Aw!" Mouse crossed her arms and huffed. "Listen up,

Lightning Bug, you'd better get working on that wish so Snow White can tell me!"

"It's Sirius," blurted Henry, and both Mouse and Snow White craned their heads to look at him.

"*Everything's* serious with you, Henry," said Mouse.

"*No*, the name of the star is Sirius."

"I already named it," said Mouse, scowling at him. "Get your own star!"

"It *has* a name. Sirius. The Dog Star."

"Stars have dogs?"

"*No*. It's part of the constellation Canis Major. You know—Canis? Dog?" Mouse looked even more confused than before, and Henry rolled his eyes, muttering, "Why do I bother?"

"Because you like us," said Snow White, sitting up across from him to cozy up to the coals.

"You do like us," said Mouse, even though Henry had not said he didn't—had not answered at all, actually. "You know you do! Or else you wouldn't be out here with us! You hate people!"

Henry occupied himself by tightening the latch on his pack. "What does that have to do with you two being completely annoying?"

"You love us!" Mouse shouted, and leapt at him, leaning

on his back with her arms wrapped around his neck. "Just admit it!"

"Watch the coals!" He pulled at her arms to keep them from choking him. "For dragon's sake, Mouse! Is there any time of day you behave like a normal human instead of a feral cat?"

Snow White laughed, then gave her friend a sly grin. "Should we tickle him, Mouse?"

"You wouldn't dare." There was a playful challenge in his eyes she was happy to see. They had broken through his hard exterior to reveal part of the Henry she had met the night of the party. The Henry who wasn't homesick and closed off from the affection of friendship.

"Tickle him, Snow White!" Mouse whooped as she climbed onto his shoulders. "I'll hold him down."

"Wait wait wait!" Henry laughed as Snow White crawled around the coals to tickle him into submission. "Okay, I like you. Okay? Jiminy crickets!"

"Just hearing you laugh is good enough for me," said Snow White as Henry wrestled Mouse from his shoulders.

He set Mouse on her feet and gave her a gentle push away from him. "Go lie down."

"I don't want to," the little girl fussed. "I want to name some more stars."

"They're all already named."

"Sirius?" Mouse gave Henry a skeptical, disapproving look as she lay back down in her spot. "That's so ugly. And it doesn't even look like a dog. I like Lightning Bug better."

Henry sighed and looked at Snow White for help. She shrugged. "I have to be honest. I like Lightning Bug better, too."

"See, Henry?" Mouse stuck her tongue out at him before settling down on her back.

"Why are you encouraging this?" Henry asked Snow White.

"There's nothing wrong with a little harmless fun," said Snow White. She thought of her birthday while she was growing up: how every year she and her parents would pick apples to bake pies for the entire kingdom. How wild and hectic it had always been . . . but what great fun everyone had, despite all the rushing around.

"Speaking of names," said Mouse, "I've been wondering, why did your parents name you Snow White?"

Snow White chuckled.

"I'm so glad she asked first," Henry said. Snow White was glad he wasn't stewing any longer. Even so, she was certain he wouldn't be answering any questions about his feelings—not that night, at least—and she would respect that and leave him be. "I didn't want to have to be the one to do it."

She laughed full out now, almost needing to stop to catch her breath. The joy of friendship . . . part of her had thought she would never get to experience that in Diamant. "Both of you are silly."

"You're named after precipitation," Henry said, smirking. "One has to wonder."

She grinned. "Well, if you must know, I was born during a snowstorm."

"That's it?" Mouse asked with a small disappointed scowl. "Why not Snowflake, then? Or Winter? Those are pretty."

"Snow White is pretty," Henry said in a chastising tone. But when he caught Snow White's gaze from across the coals, he froze. "The name, I mean."

"I happen to *love* my name," Snow White said, no offense in her tone whatsoever, "because my parents named me after the special circumstances of my birthday. And I think that's a beautiful thing."

Mouse nodded. "Well, when you say it like that, it makes sense."

"What about you, Mouse?" Snow White tickled the little girl's neck, and she giggled. "You don't look like a mouse to me."

"I'm small, that's why. I'm the only kid in Diamant, and I'll be a kid forever."

"Not forever," Snow White said reassuringly. "Not after we find the Ruby Heart. You'll get to go home and grow up and live a full life."

Mouse scrunched up her nose like a real mouse. "Didn't Tabitha tell you the truth back in town, Snow White? The Ruby Heart isn't real. I'm only here because I like you a lot, and if you were going on the quest, I was going. And it's been just as fun as I thought it would be, but there's not going to be anything on the other end."

"You truly don't think it's real?"

"I don't know." The little girl rolled onto her stomach, laid her head on her arms, and closed her eyes. "But I really like it here in Diamant. I don't have to eat my vegetables or go to bed early. I don't have to grow up and get old and wrinkly. And the gems are pretty! Why would I ever want to go back to a world without any of that?"

Snow White and Henry looked at each other. He had been right: Mouse had no desire to leave this place, and she didn't intend to. Did she not quite understand what they were journeying to? When it came down to it, how would she feel about them actually securing the Ruby Heart?

Snow White didn't want to think about that, about breaking a little girl's heart. Mouse didn't know any better; she didn't realize the real world was the best place for her. And soon enough she would realize vegetables were delicious.

"What about you, Henry?" Snow White asked, attempting to lighten the mood. "Where does your name come from?"

He seemed a little thrown off that anyone would ask him such a thing. "It's just a regular name," he said with a shrug. "It's nothing special."

"It is very special. After all, you're attached to it."

Henry blushed, looking at the coals. "I was named after my father. And his father, and his. I'm the fourth Henry in my family."

"Henry the fourth," said Snow White. "See? That *is* special. A family name."

"And at least there are only four," said Mouse. "You're not like Henry the eighth or something annoying like that."

"Okay," said Henry, sighing at Mouse's exaggeration, "that's quite enough from you for one day. Good night, Mouse."

"I don't want to sleep," Mouse complained, and then immediately yawned.

"We have a long way to walk tomorrow. From here to the second trial it's uphill, literally."

"We can do it," said Snow White, determined. "We've made it this far, after all. Only two trials to go."

Henry nodded and positioned himself to lie down. "Good night, Stardrop."

Snow White smiled. As much as she knew she had to sleep, she wanted the night to last. The comradery, the sweet conversation and friendship. What she wouldn't give to keep that moment, that feeling forever.

But her mind interrupted her heart. She could never stay there. Her kingdom needed her. She valued the friendships she had formed there, but it wasn't real life. In real life they were all in trouble, in need.

As much as she loved that moment, the second trial awaited. And after how exhausting the journey had been thus far, Snow White had a feeling it was only going to get more and more difficult.

Still, there was no reason to think of that now, not when she needed sleep. There was no reason to think of it ever, actually, because no amount of hardship would ever bring down her mood. Not while her heart was so full of love and hope.

"Good night, Henry," she said, and snuggled up near the coals.

Snow White felt herself dreaming and wished desperately on the stars to wake.

She was in the sky, moving rapidly through the air as if flying. When she looked down, she saw all of Diamant, like a kaleidoscope of color, a massive piece of stained glass as far as the eye could see. But her shoulders were hurting. . . . Why were her shoulders hurting?

A terrible, monstrous caw broke the sky in two to reveal a gaping hole, and when Snow White looked up, she saw she was being carried by a massive beast—a crow, like the ones they had encountered that day, except far too big to be anything but a monster. It carried her with its claws dug into her shoulders.

And when she looked around, she saw multiple crows, each carrying one of her seven friends . . . and Jonathan. One by one, the crows dropped her friends into the water below, and her screams for them were cut off by the crows' manic cawing.

Suddenly, the bird holding her let go, and Snow White fell like a lightning bolt into the water. She dropped like a stone, deep beneath the icy waters. As she swam toward the surface, she saw the massive crow flying above the water, its wings outstretched. And at the water's edge stood the Queen, smiling wickedly down at her as Snow White fought to swim to the surface. The sinister pair was quickly joined by the crow's murder, the monstrous birds filling the space until the water was shadowed and murky. *Let me out!* Snow White wanted to scream, but found she couldn't breach the surface, with the crows pushing her under whenever she tried, disorienting her, screeching at her, plunging her into the depths until she could no longer fight, until she could no longer—

Snow White gasped for breath as her eyes snapped open to stare at the moon overhead. No monstrous crows. No water. She was exactly where she'd fallen asleep, under the stars beside her friends. She let out a heavy breath in both relief and frustration. She'd never had nightmares like that before arriving in Diamant, and it was clear the Queen meant to torment her.

A quiet snoring drew her attention, and she looked over to see Mouse curled up where she'd left her. Henry, too, was still sleeping, lying on his back with his arms folded across his stomach. She was thankful, at least, that her friends weren't plagued by nightmares.

Or rather . . . visions.

That was what it was called when a dream displayed the future, was it not? A vision. And she'd had one the night before, full of crystals and wickedness . . . and then the next day, Henry had been caught almost exactly as she had foreseen. Would he have been covered by crystal, a living statue, if she hadn't acted in time?

Snow White shivered, hugging herself against the night's chill. When she lifted her head, she saw that the coals had burned down to next to nothing. She sighed, exhausted but too cold to just lie there, too on edge from her dream to go back to sleep and risk falling into another nightmare. She pushed herself up and crawled to Henry's pack. She had shifted the pack only the smallest bit, enough to make the coals inside knock against each other, when Henry jolted awake.

"Hey," he murmured. He propped himself up on his elbow. "Can't sleep?"

"It's just a little chilly," she said, rubbing her arms. "Don't worry about me. I can handle the coals. You can go back to sleep."

"I'll do it." He reached for his pack and dragged it to

himself, then leaned on his stomach and elbows to fish out fresh coals.

Snow White watched him work for a moment as he added fresh coals to the embers, replenishing their warmth. "I had a nightmare," she said.

"Do you want to talk about it?" Henry asked.

"I . . ." She hesitated. She shook her head. It seemed too far-fetched to even entertain. Yet Henry's tone of companionship encouraged her. "I think we *should* talk about it. Because my last one came true."

Henry paused in his work to look at her. "What do you mean, 'came true'?"

"I dreamed about being covered head to toe in gems. And then, the next day, you stepped into that crystal trap."

Henry looked at her as if he didn't understand a word of what she had said. "Okay."

"Tonight I dreamed that I was dropped in water by giant crows . . . and I never came up to the surface."

"But that already happened today," said Henry, and he seemed a little relieved that he could make some sense of what she was telling him. "The water, the crows. Except you *did* surface. Those crows must have frightened you more than you realized."

"I suppose," Snow White said.

"I wouldn't read into it too much. Dreams like that happen when you're in stressful situations with not enough rest. Trust me. I used to have those all the time when I first arrived in Diamant. They'll eventually pass."

Snow White nodded. "It makes sense when you put it that way. Thank you, Henry."

"Sure thing," he said, doing a last-minute check on the coals. They were burning warm enough to last them the rest of the night. And then he hesitated, poised between lying back down and moving closer to her. "Do you . . . need a hug or something?" he asked awkwardly.

Snow White pressed her lips together to hold back a laugh; she didn't want to risk waking Mouse. "That's sweet of you to offer," she said. "But I think I'll be all right."

"Okay, then . . ." Henry looked a little sheepish as he lay back down, shifting his pack to lie on it like a pillow. "I'll see you in the morning."

"Yes, tomorrow is a new day," Snow White said, lying down on her side. And she hoped beyond hope as she closed her eyes that no more dreams would disturb her sleep.

The three travel companions awoke with renewed energy at first light. The sky was smeared with a sunrise of bright oranges and golden yellows fading into soft pinks. It looked like a painting and was more beautiful than any hue of gemstone.

After her vision the night before, Snow White made up her mind that she would be careful not to touch anything outside the path—including anything crows might covet and bodies of water. They didn't need anything else to delay their journey to the second trial. And they certainly did not need to run into anything else that would put them in danger.

The path was unusually cruel; the incline made it twice as difficult. They were traveling uphill gradually at first, but it wasn't long before that changed, with the three of them having to lean forward to stay upright. It was clear they were headed not simply uphill, but up a mountain.

At the steepest incline, the three of them were crawling on hands and knees to keep from sliding down. It didn't help that the sun had risen higher and grew hotter the higher they climbed. With no trees to shade them, it was as if they were beneath a magnifying glass and the sun's heat was focusing on them.

Finally, they reached the peak of the incline, which leveled off into an area of grassy land and trees. The sound of racing, crashing water, a low rumble in the distance, filled the space. As they made their way through the trees, the sound of the rapids grew louder and a stone wall rose higher and higher in front of them. After about a mile, the trees cleared.

When they had walked as far as they could, Henry studied the map.

"This can't be right," he murmured.

Mouse threw her hands up in the air. "I told you that map wasn't magic!"

"It's not the map," he said irritably. "Look."

They stood on a cliff, twenty or more feet above a ravine with a river that flowed rapidly through it, crashing against the rocks within it and echoing up the rocky walls. And though the map had promised what looked to be a sturdy bridge that led across the dangerous rapids to another cliff, in actuality it was quite a different story: where a stone bridge was marked on the map, there was instead a rickety old bridge held together by tattered ropes . . . that led to nothing but a solid rock face covered in emerald ivy.

"Perhaps we climb up the wall once we get across," Snow White suggested.

"The map clearly says the bridge will take us to the other side." Henry looked closer at it, from multiple angles, even turning the map upside down to make sure. "There shouldn't be anything to climb."

"I don't like that map," Mouse grumbled.

"Well, let's just think for a second," said Snow White. "Remember the last trial? We didn't know what it was until we stepped into the field."

"The second trial is supposed to give you the key to the Ruby Heart," said Mouse. "That's what a lot of people said their second trial was. But there's nowhere over there to keep a key."

"Well," said Henry, tucking the map into his pocket

and setting his pack on the ground, "let's go and see, shall we?" He held his hand up to Snow White. "And by 'let's,' I mean me."

"I don't want to go on that shabby bridge, anyway," Mouse grumbled, taking a few steps back.

"I thought you said there were no exceptions for princesses, Henry," said Snow White, raising her brows at him. "Besides, we're in this together."

"My caring whether or not you fall to your death has nothing to do with your being a princess. Besides, it's too narrow for both of us, anyway."

"It *is* too narrow for both of us," Snow White agreed even as she eyed Henry's frame, which was much larger than hers and undoubtedly much heavier. But it was hard to tell Henry anything contrary to something he was determined about.

Henry took hold of the ropes on either side of the bridge, and already it was rocking before he even stepped onto it. Carefully, he lowered a foot onto the first slab, and the crack and snap it made echoed through Snow White's entire body. It must have alarmed Henry, too, as he stumbled back to safety.

"That didn't sound good," Snow White said, trying to steady her racing heart.

"It didn't feel good, either. That slab nearly snapped right under my foot." He chewed on his lip. "I'm too heavy for it."

"I can do it," Snow White said, determined.

"It's too dangerous," Henry and Mouse said in unison.

"I know it is, but I'm also smaller than you," she said to Henry, touching his arm. "And after I test it as you did, if it doesn't want to hold, we'll think of something else."

If the map said this was the second trial, then it must be the second trial. Perhaps, as for the first, it would have to be their perspective that was adjusted rather than the location.

Henry hesitated before nodding. "I'll be right here to snatch you away from it if need be."

Snow White shook her head. "You really do worry so much, Henry."

But as soon as she stepped up to the bridge, she was beginning to worry she had made the wrong decision, too. The bridge was suspended *higher* than it had appeared from a safer distance. She glanced back up at her destination quickly. *Pick a spot on the wall. Don't look away from it. Everything will be fine.*

She took a deep breath . . . and took her first step.

The first slab creaked as her weight settled on it, and

she jolted from the shock of quick movement as Henry grabbed her arm.

She whipped her head to look at him. "Henry!"

"I'm just making sure."

"You scared me half to death."

"Well, *sorry*, I thought you were going to *fall* to your death." His cheeks flamed as he released her arm.

Mouse giggled from her spot of safety.

"The slab is fine," Snow White said, more for her own assurance than anything else. "I can do this."

They looked at each other for a moment, their nerves and fears swirling together. But there would be no progress if they stood still—no Ruby Heart, no going home, no saving Snow White's kingdom.

"Henry," she said gently, "it's all right."

Finally, he nodded in return.

All she had to do was get to the other side. That didn't seem so very hard. She took another careful step, then another. The bridge creaked with each step but held beneath her. Still, the ropes wobbled, and she clung to them tighter, looking steadily at the wall before her.

But had the bridge always been this long? It had looked shorter from the flat, safe land. With each step it seemed as if the bridge stretched longer and—

Her heart caught in her throat as her foot missed a slab, and she barely heard Henry cry her name and Mouse's little scream as she grabbed for the ropes. "I'm okay!" she called out, but she wasn't sure that was true; she was in the middle of a rickety bridge, suspended what seemed like miles and miles above a river, and had no idea if she could manage to get off her knees and back onto her feet to cross.

"Come back, Snow White," Henry called. "We'll figure out another way."

"I'm halfway there," she called back, or she thought she did—but her heart was pounding loudly in her ears.

And her head spun as she looked down at the raging water below.

"You don't have to pretend to be brave," called Mouse. "It's not worth you dying, Snow White!"

Pretend to be brave . . .

Her father had been brave. It was one of the things she had admired most about him before he had gone away. . . . No. Before he had been taken from her.

But she was her father's daughter. And if he could be brave, so could she.

Snow White took a deep breath. She didn't try to stand on the unstable bridge. Instead, she lay on her stomach and pulled herself along. She grabbed the slabs in front of her, pulled, grabbed, pulled. Fortunately, she made faster progress than when she had been on her feet, despite being able to see far too much of the river this way. But she was getting there. . . . She was almost there.

Finally, she made it to the wall. Only then did she attempt to stand, using the emerald vines and precious stones protruding from the wall to help her instead of messing with the flimsy rope. She heard her friends shouting, but at that distance she couldn't understand much of what they were saying.

Except for *You did it!*

Because she had done it. She was one step closer to the Ruby Heart. One step closer to saving her kingdom.

And then she stumbled as her arm fell forward into the wall. As the vines parted, Snow White realized she was staring into the dimness of a shallow hole in the wall. No, not a hole—a shelf. It was cut out neatly, intentionally, in an angular fashion. And resting on the shelf was a box made of smoothed gemstone in swirling blues and greens. It looked like some sort of jewelry box.

So Mouse had been right about the second trial. This box was too smooth and polished, too deliberately placed to contain anything but what they needed for the next trial.

Snow White was positive it contained the key required to unlock the Ruby Heart.

"There's a box in here!" she called to her friends. She took hold of the round handle on top, lifting up the weighty lid slowly, carefully. It fit on the box so snuggly that she had to inch it up, keeping it level so one side wouldn't rise before the other and get stuck. When it finally came loose, it let out a ringing vibration that rumbled through Snow White's arm and the stone shelf surrounding it. Like a victory bell.

Snow White released a deep breath, setting the lid aside just as carefully. She leaned forward to look inside the box and saw . . . nothing? But that couldn't be right. No, of course not. It was shady inside the hole, with only a few glints of sunlight making their way through the vines, and her shadow had to be further dimming it, tricking her mind. She reached inside the box, feeling around every corner, her heart pounding harder. Nothing. She tipped it to better look inside. Still nothing.

"There's no key in here!" she called over her shoulder.

No key. A box, but no key. Had someone already taken it or accidentally dropped it into the ravine?

Or maybe . . . maybe there had never been a key in the first place.

"Stardrop!" Henry called. "I felt the earth move. Get back over here, now!"

But his warning came too late as the rumble went through the wall once again, this time strong enough to send a crack climbing up the wall, strong enough to shake the bridge. Snow White grabbed on to the wall and the emerald vines, quickly shutting the box. She knew she had felt something when she had opened the box; maybe shutting it would—

"Snow White!"

The ground shook again, and as she turned around, she stumbled and fell face-first onto the bridge, where she held on for dear life as it rocked and shook like a fishing boat in a storm. When she ventured a look up to check on her friends, they were having as hard a time staying on their feet as she was. Was this the trial? Maybe all they had to do was hold on until it passed.

But then she watched in horror as rocks began to fall down the side of the high wall. She braced herself against the bridge in anticipation of being crushed. Instead, the rocks bounced off the wall, pummeling the ground where her friends stood. It didn't make sense—nothing made sense here—but that was the least important fact now. She had to get across the bridge again, as much as it was shaking, as much as she—

"Watch out!" she cried. But her warning was in vain as Henry shoved Mouse out of the way of a falling rock only to lose his own footing. She heard herself scream his name as he fell over the edge into the racing water below.

Snow White wasn't about to lose Henry to that river. She couldn't. They were in this together. She took a breath and leapt off the bridge, hanging there for a moment like a bird in flight caught by the wind before diving into the void below.

9

Snow White's intention had been to dive into the water—preferably gracefully and without slamming into one of the many rocks below—catch up to Henry, and pull him out to safety.

The river had other ideas.

Snow White crashed into the water, the cold of it sending a shock through her body that made it hard to even catch her breath. The river immediately began to drag her along mercilessly before she could try to swim, tumbling her like laundry or a ship in a storm. She managed to get to the surface and let out a desperate gasp, struggling to keep her head above water, to look for Henry. Heaven forbid he had hit his head on a rock or gotten sucked underwater, unable to find air.

"Henry!" Snow White called, barely finishing his name before the racing water slammed her into a rock.

Her vision went blank, as if she was looking into an abyss. For a moment, her mind drifted, and she closed her eyes. Everything was quiet, muted and peaceful, as if she was submerged in calm water instead of rapids. She opened her eyes and found herself under the surface, watching the water churn slowly around her, far too slowly to be really happening. Rays of sunlight streamed through the multitude of bubbles.

She tried to swim, but her limbs would not so much as move. *I'm drowning,* she thought suddenly. It was the only clear thought she had in her head.

Give in, she felt a voice say.

The bubbles swirled around her, like a vortex trying to suck the air from her very lungs—air she barely felt she had. The bubbles circled her, strangely predatory in their movements, until they were no longer bubbles . . . until they shifted form, blending together into the loose figure of a woman, transparent and lacking all detail. Like a mirage.

This isn't real, Snow White thought. *I can't stay here—*

Give in.

Suddenly, black ink burst from each of the bubbles, shifting as the mirage changed form again, the movement of the water tightening Snow White's chest.

You're killing me, she tried to scream, but she only took in a mouthful of water as the ink shifted again, forming a more solid structure with hate-filled eyes she recognized.

Those eyes seemed to make the water press into Snow White harder. She grabbed her throat, her consciousness drifting, the water pressing down on her, overtaking her. . . .

And the Queen smiled like a vicious beast, her teeth as razor-sharp as any wolf's.

Give in, Snow White—

"This isn't real!" Snow White heard herself shout. She blinked, and the horrible creature—the Queen—was gone. Snow White's head was above the surface again, and she heard herself coughing, recovering. She had caught against that rock she had slammed into, the water rushing at her, pressing her into it and keeping her from drifting away. Her head ached because of that, but she would worry about that later. There was no time to think of anything else when Henry had been in the water far too long and . . . What if he was unconscious? How far must he have been carried downriver?

"Henry!" she called, barely hearing her own voice above the rapids.

"Here!" she thought she heard, and when she turned, she spotted him clinging to a rock ahead of her.

She moved away from her rock to let the river take her, then fought and kicked, trying to put herself in the right position to make it to Henry. He held out his hand, and they grabbed each other just before she flowed past him. She kicked and he pulled, and they clung to each other and the rock. Snow White panted, trying not to think about the fact that she had nearly drowned a moment before. That the Queen had even tried to encourage it. If she died in Diamant, she would be gone in the real world, too.

And too many people needed her back home for that sort of nonsense to happen.

"It's too dangerous to swim it," Snow White gasped.

"Agreed," Henry said, breathless. "And I've already wasted too much strength trying."

"Don't let go." It was one thing to say it, but her own grip was weakening, slipping. Still, she clung to him and the rock like they were lifelines. "There has to be a way to shore."

Henry's grip on her started to loosen, and Snow White could see his arms trembling as he tried to keep hold.

"Don't give up, Henry," she said, feeling panicked—not

about the water, not for herself, but about the possibility of losing her friend to the ruthless rapids if he gave in to exhaustion, if he lost his strength. Snow White ventured to peer around the rock. There had to be *something* that could help them. But all she saw ahead was endless water and more rocks. Then it hit her.

"We can drift from rock to rock," she shouted over the water.

Henry looked at Snow White as if she had lost her mind. "What?"

"There are rocks that get closer and closer to shore. If we let the river take us to each one, one at a time, it will push us in the direction of the shore."

"But there are rocks underneath, too. We can't control which way we'll flow."

"You have to trust me, Henry." She felt her grip weakening even more, her own hands now shaking—though she couldn't tell if she was shivering from weakness or the cold water. "You see that rock up ahead? The one to the right."

Henry's teeth chattered, but he managed a nod. "I see it."

"We just have to get to that rock," said Snow White. "When I say go, we let the current take us. Ready?"

"Absolutely not."

"Go!"

They kept hold of each other as the current whipped them away, far more quickly than Snow White had expected. Still, they managed to grab their target, smacking against the stone and nearly losing their grip.

"We can't sustain this," said Henry, gritting his teeth.

Grabbing on to the second rock had taken more energy than she had expected. "Be brave, Henry. Don't lose hope."

Her words seemed to knock a little more courage into Henry, because he shook his head and looked forward. "That one—with the flat top?"

It was the exact one she had been eyeing; he understood the plan. "Ready?" she said.

"Go!"

They allowed themselves to be dragged from rock to rock, weakening each time they were slammed against one but refusing to give in to fatigue and pain from the cold water and sharp rocks against their fingers. Finally, they were close enough to taste the shore—if there hadn't been sharp rocks along it preventing them from flowing directly to it. But if they could manage to stand on top of one last rock, they could make a small leap to the shore. To safety.

That is, if they had the strength.

They made sure they were on the side of the rock where the river pushed them into it instead of away. And then Snow White took a deep breath and reached her arms on top to pull herself up. Henry gripped the back of her dress to give her a small boost. She wiggled and crawled and dragged herself—looking dignified wasn't a priority at a time like this, only staying alive was—until she was lying on her stomach on top the rock.

She was tired, but there was no time to rest just then. Henry had boosted her up. Now it was her turn.

She knelt on the rock and reached for Henry's hand. Her heart skipped as it nearly slipped out of her grasp before she snatched it back with both hands. They looked at each other, realizing what had almost happened . . . realizing they both would have been undone if it had.

"Don't let go," she said as much for herself as for him. She pulled him up while he crawled and climbed as she had, until he was kneeling on the rock. They gripped each other's arms, trembling, unsteady. But alive.

And far too close to safety to give up.

They helped each other to their feet, then gripped hands as they leapt to shore, where their exhausted knees promptly collapsed beneath them.

"Are you okay?" Henry panted.

Snow White could barely answer she was so fatigued, but she managed a soft "mm-hm."

But was she? She wasn't sure. Because she had almost drowned. Just like in her dream. This place—or rather, the Queen—seemed determined not only to make sure she would never wake up from the poison apple's sleep, but to destroy her completely.

"You're bleeding," Henry frowned as he looked at her.

Snow White pressed a finger to her tender temple and winced. "I'm all right. Those rocks were brutal, but it could have been far worse."

She leaned up on her elbows to look around. If this world had been made from plants, as it ought to have been, the place they were in might have been an oasis. But all Snow White could see was the high stone wall on the other side of the river, and the high cliff behind them.

"Was that the trial?" Snow White asked finally.

"I don't know," said Henry. He groaned as he got to his feet.

They were far from the bridge—that was for certain—but they could only know how far when they had strength enough to walk around the river bend. Behind them, in the face of the cliff, was a large opening to a cavern. It must have been deep, because Snow White couldn't see the back wall; the low sun of the approaching evening added to the lurking shadows within. Part of her didn't care to see to the back wall and find out they weren't alone. The sky was beginning to gray a little, which seemed to match the mood of the moment. Still, Snow White was determined not to let anything affect her hope.

"Do we risk the cavern or the climb?" Henry murmured, assessing both choices carefully as he looked from one to the other.

"Snow White! Henry!" Mouse called. She must have just caught up with them running along the cliff with her small legs. "You're okay!"

Snow White and Henry looked up to see Mouse's head peeking over the cliff. It reminded Snow White of the moment when they had first met and she had been peeking around the corner with bright curious eyes.

"We're safe!" Snow White called up to her.

"Stay there! I'll run back to town to get help!" And her dark hair flashed out of sight before either of them could respond.

"Do you even know the way?" Henry called, but she didn't respond—presumably already running back the way they had come. "Wait a second, we have the map!"

Snow White looked at Henry as he hung his head back to glare at the sky for a moment before he let out a frustrated sound.

"She'll be all right," she said, her tone encouraging. "After all, she's been here longer than anyone."

Henry rolled his eyes. "She's going to get distracted before she even makes it down the mountain."

Snow White paused. *Possibly. Okay, more than likely.* But there was no need for her to be as negative as Henry, so she settled on "Nonsense. She knows this is an emergency."

"We're going to be stuck down here for a week."

"Have a little faith, Henry."

Henry's expression looked as if he had no intention of doing so. "Why would the trial lead us to nothing, do you think?" he said, as if trying to work it out for himself.

"Well, there was supposed to be a key," said Snow White with a shrug. "I'm not sure what the next step is if we can't find it."

"*Was* there supposed to be a key? How do we even know that? Because Mouse said others had found it—" His brown eyes widened slightly, and he snapped his fingers a few times. "Others found a key. *Multiple people* found keys. So wouldn't they have brought them when they came back? Where did all those keys go?"

"You're making my head spin, Henry," Snow White said, chuckling.

"Well, don't you see? Maybe a key wasn't the point. Maybe a physical key had nothing to do with anything."

"So what was the point, then?" she asked.

Henry paused, the light in his eyes burning out the slightest bit. He shrugged. "Still trying to figure that out."

He headed into the cavern before them, and Snow White followed; she had been wary of it, but if she could survive a raging river, a cavern would be nothing—even if she was more than certain that, judging by what they had encountered so far, there was something dangerous in the depths of it.

"I don't think there's a hidden meaning," she said. "Either someone took it or Mouse was mistaken."

Henry rolled his eyes. "Mouse was mistaken, all right. I should never have allowed a child on a quest." He settled down, leaning against the jewel wall of the cavern. "Still, I'm glad she was here to go for help. We don't have the gear to climb out of here alone."

"You see?" said Snow White, sitting beside him and shoving his shoulder playfully. "Children are made for quests."

Henry grumbled, though he didn't specifically disagree.

Suddenly, they both froze. Had someone . . . screamed? Snow White could have sworn she had heard an echoing from the cavern. And it didn't help that Henry was looking in that direction as well. He clearly must have heard the same thing she had.

And then a bird flew out from the darkness, screeching as it went. Snow White's nerves eased as it flew over their heads and out into the sky.

"Just a bird," Henry murmured.

Birds weren't exactly safe to be around there, but Snow White thought it better not to bring up the negative aspects of their journey.

Henry sighed heavily, as if the sound had stressed his nerves as much as hers. And then he got up and wandered forward, looking into the expanse of the dark tunnel. After wringing out her skirts, Snow White followed. It was far too dark in there, and it was not the time for the two of them to get separated.

"Where do you think it leads?" she asked.

"I don't know, but it feels heavy in here, you know? Haunted."

It was clear Henry was feeling the same uneasiness about the tunnel as she was. Except to her, it didn't feel haunted—it just felt *wrong*. Still, they needed shelter and didn't have many choices at the moment. "There's no such thing as ghosts," she assured him.

"No such thing as ghosts?" Henry scoffed "You have clearly not seen enough of the world, Stardrop."

"Why are you trying to scare me, Henry?" she asked. She again gave him a gentle shove as if pushing a lever to make him stop. "We have to sleep in here, and you're talking about malevolent spirits coming to get us."

"I'm just preparing you. This place is—" Henry stumbled a bit, kicking over a small slab of gemstone that had been propped up on a rock. He bent down to pick it up and held it for both of them to see. The two travel companions froze when they saw what was carved into the face of it. It was hard to see due to the lack of light, but Snow White was certain it read, *Beware, All Who Enter Here.*

"Okay." Henry dropped the crudely made sign and backed away from it, looking around quickly. It was obvious he was forcing his voice not to sound panicked. "You were saying?"

"That sign could be nothing but a bluff to keep people out. I'm sure there's no real threat in here," Snow White said, her thin voice barely convincing to her own ears.

"There have been threats all along the way, and you think the creepy cave is going to be safer?" Henry said, stating exactly what Snow White knew and didn't want to admit.

Was it too late to find a different shelter? The quickly setting sun said yes. They retreated closer to the opening of the cavern, away from the dark tunnel and, hopefully, the threat of any ghosts.

Henry directed his energy fueled by fright and anxiety into digging some coal out of his pack and roughly piling it. "Well, I won't be getting any sleep tonight."

Snow White sat beside him, watching him organize the coal.

"We'll be safe on this side of the cavern, I'm sure," she said, her voice hopeful, even if she did eye the dark tunnel.

He nodded. "Staying together will help, certainly, and as long as we keep track of danger from both the tunnel side and the cavern opening, we'll be fine." He seemed to say that sarcastically, but Snow White chose to ignore his tone. "And then tomorrow we'll figure out a way out of here and head back to town."

Snow White gaped, her tone concerned when she asked, "Head back to town?"

"Look at us," he said, gesturing to their dark surroundings. "We barely got through the first trial without being eaten by wolves, we were nearly killed by multiple traps, and—in case you forgot about the whole rockslide and river incident—we just failed the second trial miserably. We might as well go back before something irreversibly horrible happens."

Snow White studied his hunched shoulders, his downcast eyes. It was clear he had given up hope, and she couldn't let him continue on that way. "We're going to find the Ruby Heart. We're going to go home, Henry. I know it."

He took out his flint, then changed his mind about using it. "If you'd been here as long as I have," he replied, "perhaps you wouldn't be so hopeful."

"There is no time limit for hope. It never has to run out as far as I'm concerned." *Still* . . . She tucked her knees up and wrapped her arms around them. "But how long have you been here, exactly?" she asked.

He scoffed. "Too long."

Thunder rumbled, loud and close, and a sudden breeze swooped in. A drizzle quickly followed, and Snow White watched as it turned to rain just as swiftly before becoming a noisy downpour. When things occurred in Diamant, they certainly took place very quickly.

"Of course," Henry grumbled. He lit the coals. Fortunately, the rain wasn't entering the cavern, but there was a bit of a chill swirling in. The cold crawled quickly through Snow White's body. The night, the rain, and her wet clothing made it feel like the temperature had dropped significantly.

The two of them huddled near the burning coals, trying to ease their shivers.

When Henry stopped talking, Snow White patted his shoulder reassuringly. "I just want to understand, Henry. How long have you been here that you would have lost all hope?"

Henry took a deep breath, as if this was the second hardest thing he had ever had to confess—the first being his yearning for home. "Going on five years now."

Snow White rubbed her face to hide her momentary gape. What a terrible thing to be stuck in a place like this for so long.

"How do you think the enchantment affects us in the real world?" he asked. "Do you think our bodies age normally, even if we look the same age in our subconscious? Or are our bodies frozen in time?"

Snow White had never thought of that aspect of it; she'd been so focused on getting home that she had never considered being there for more than a few days.

In her silence, Henry sighed. "I suppose it doesn't matter anyway. I'll never see that life again."

"The rain has got you feeling blue, that's all." Snow White linked arms with him—to comfort him and also because it helped a bit against the cold. "How many of these journeys have you been on? Perhaps we can compare them and discover a pattern in the trials."

He scoffed, then thought about it for a moment. He was silent, holding on to his flint absently. "I stopped keeping track after twenty trips . . . mostly because I didn't see the point in memorializing my failures."

"You told me yourself the map and trials change depending on the person. There's no sense in giving yourself a hard time over something you can't control."

"I guess so," Henry muttered.

Snow White chewed on her lip. "It feels so long ago now, but . . . remember when I asked you what you did before Diamant?" she asked hesitantly. "Do you feel like answering now?"

"Now that we're trapped in a cave and I can't escape this conversation?" Henry sighed.

Perhaps she was being too pushy. But Henry gave her a soft smile, which was such an improvement in his mood that Snow White was glad she had ventured to change the subject.

"I wanted to be a knight before all this," Henry said. "A royal guard, actually. One of the elites."

Snow White sat up to look at him curiously. "But I thought you said you worked with gemstones."

"Well . . ." He rubbed the back of his neck, embarrassed. "I only *wanted* to be a knight. Really I was just a blacksmith's apprentice. We'd get a lot of commissions to make swords for nobles, and they always wanted elaborate hilts with different gemstones embedded in them."

"How wonderful." Snow White was awed by his words. "That's why you're so familiar with what everything is made of here."

"And why I know how to use a sword. I'd test them out, to check their balance. Usually, I'd make some excuse to test them longer than necessary to get even more practice in."

"You'd make a wonderful knight, Henry," Snow White said lightly. "You have such a naturally protective way about you."

Henry looked surprised. "Really?"

"Granted, you would be a very grumpy one."

That, at least, got a chuckle out of him.

"But you're also a wonderful blacksmith," said Snow

White. "I saw you making something the other night. And if you made your sword and Tabitha's pickaxe, well, then I would say you are far too skilled to continue calling yourself an apprentice."

"What is this, Compliment Henry Night?" Henry asked with mock offense to cover his embarrassment. "Let's change the subject."

"Well, it's all true, isn't it? You've been smithing blades the entire five years you've lived here. You have far exceeded the title of apprentice."

Henry chuckled. "Well, thank you, but . . ." He shook his head and grinned at her. "Is it your turn to be embarrassed now, Stardrop? What about you? What was life like for you before you were sent here?"

"I was . . ." Snow White took a deep breath. How could she ever explain everything that had happened just before she arrived in Diamant? *My evil stepmother tried to kill me multiple times to continue ruling my kingdom with an iron fist.*

She cringed.

"When I was little," she began, watching the embers inside the coals shift and smolder, "and my mother was still alive . . ." *And my father.* She swallowed back the recent awful memory. "Every year on my birthday, my parents and I would pick apples from the orchard and bake pies for the entire kingdom. It's my favorite memory of my child-hood, those moments when we weren't just rulers of our kingdom, but friends with everyone who lived there. When kindness was ruler, really, instead of the fear the Queen instills. . . ."

She felt tears at the edges of her eyes. She had tried her hardest to keep the moment light, yet all she could think of was how much she missed her parents. How much she wished her kingdom didn't have to suffer. How much she wished she could go home.

How much longer would it take Mouse to return with help? How much longer would her people have to wait for her to set things right? She wanted to save her friends as soon as possible and hated the idea of them waiting, hoping for someone to help them, wondering if she'd ever wake up.

Finally, she looked at Henry, only to find him gaping.

"What's wrong?" she said, concern overtaking her.

"Did you say you and your parents were . . . *rulers* of the kingdom?"

Snow White shrugged. "*Ruler* really is a cold, distant word for it."

"Okay, but I'd been calling you a princess ironically. Are you saying you're an *actual* princess?"

"Um—" She blinked, a bit flustered by the shock in his

tone. "Yes. I suppose. The Queen has never made me feel like one."

Henry raised his brows. "The *Queen* is your *mother?*"

"Stepmother."

"These are all important details you oddly neglected to tell me," said Henry, so agitated that for a moment he fumbled for words. "I mean . . . cauldrons! I should be bowing to you and—"

"No, please don't." Snow White smiled. "I like just having friends without all that complication. I like having people I can truly be myself with."

"Be yourself . . ." Henry poked at the coals a little with his sword, shifting them. He stared at them a moment. "That's one thing that's hard to do in Diamant."

"What do you mean?"

"Being yourself. Voicing your true thoughts. Because we're stuck here. . . . I don't know. I feel like I can't say certain things to the others in town. I feel like they'll judge me for thinking differently."

"Is that why you use the Forgetting Stone? To feel like you fit in?"

He hesitated, then nodded. For a moment they watched the rain in silence as it threatened to drown the world in its violence.

"Is this because you're trying to escape Diamant and so many people in town don't seem to be concerned with that?" Snow White touched Henry's hand when he didn't answer. "You said that you wanted to go home," she continued, pressing him. "That you didn't think you had anything to go back to, but you wanted it anyway."

He dropped his gaze to the coals again, clearly unable to look at her as his face grew hot with shame. "I'm pretty sure I asked you not to bring this up again."

"I want you to know that there's nothing wrong with wanting to go home."

"It's a childish thought," he replied stiffly.

Snow White squeezed his hand. "I miss my home, my friends, my kingdom. I miss the smell of nature. I miss apple pie. It's not childish to want something you've lost, Henry. It's human."

She paused to see what he had to say, but for a long moment he didn't speak. She didn't rush him; she simply let him reflect on his thoughts and collect his words. And then he said, "I always hoped the Ruby Heart was real. I'd gone on so many trips, with anyone who wanted to go, but they all ended in disappointment. In nothing. And eventually, it was clear that everyone in town had settled into this place, as if it's their true home—even my own sister—and

I . . . hadn't. And to make it all worse, anytime I would bring it up, they'd look at me as if I'd lost my mind."

Henry stared at the coals without truly seeing them. "That's why I never talk about it. I have to feel normal in some way."

"It's good to talk about things, Henry," said Snow White, grabbing his shoulder reassuringly. "I'm glad you're talking to me. It helps me know how I can encourage you."

Henry scoffed. "Of course you would say that."

"To give up hope will be the beginning of the end. We can't give up. We have to keep trying."

"But what if it's not there?" Henry's voice was suddenly more distressed than Snow White had ever heard it before; a fear and hopelessness in his eyes made her want to hug him. "I've never gotten this far in the trials before. What if there is no Ruby Heart and this is all just a trick devised by the Queen to toy with us? What if it all really just leads to nothing?"

Snow White considered his words. That *did* seem like something the Queen would do. After all, hadn't she attempted to destroy Snow White since she'd arrived? The nightmare she had had that first night couldn't have been a coincidence. The Queen had poisoned all those wolves with those thorns, turning them vicious and violent. And then, in the river, when Snow White had slammed into that rock, she must have been knocked unconscious . . . and the Queen had done her very best to drown her.

It was more than obvious that the Queen was doing her best to keep anyone from finding their way home.

Henry opened his mouth but shut it quickly. He shook his head, obviously seeing no point in continuing the topic. "This cold is merciless. I'll put more coals on."

"I'll get them," said Snow White. She reached for his bag and dragged it to her, but the first things she touched inside it weren't large and slightly misshapen. No . . . they were small and round and smooth. She recognized the feel but couldn't quite believe what she was touching until she gently closed her fingers around something and took it out.

She gasped. Because she held up the pearl necklace she had gifted Henry the night they danced.

She wiped a bit of the soot off to reveal the iridescence beneath and then looked at Henry, who once again seemed embarrassed.

"You kept it," Snow White said. "After Mouse told me she lost the necklace she had made, I was worried. I thought perhaps you had—I don't know—tossed it aside somewhere. That you didn't care for the sentiment."

"I wouldn't do that," Henry said, hugging himself

nervously. "You gave it to me, after all. It was a sweet gesture. And we're . . . friends." He said it awkwardly, as if he wasn't sure he was supposed to.

"It just makes me so happy to know that you kept it." Snow White smiled, relieved. "Will you wear it now?"

Henry nodded. "How can I refuse a request like that?"

Snow White reached up and put it over his head, then adjusted it to lie straight against his chest. "Made with love and friendship, from me to you."

Henry chuckled. "I appreciate it. Thank you."

"You're welcome," Snow White said, smiling. "That's what friends are for."

"Speaking of friends . . ." His expression turned sheepish. "I've been brainstorming an alternate plan, but . . . now my idea just feels *wrong*, especially knowing that you're a real princess."

"We've both been very vulnerable with each other tonight, Henry," said Snow White. "How awful could it possibly be?"

"Not so much awful as impertinent, I think. . . ." He chewed on his lip. "I don't know if anyone told you, but there is another way to get home."

"Tabitha did mention something. True love's kiss?" Snow White asked. Henry's response to that startled her.

She had never before seen someone look so flustered over three little words. Even his ears burned red. "But it's impossible. There's no way to communicate with our loved ones in the waking world to let them know about it."

"That may be true," said Henry. He hesitated. "But there is the possibility that you don't have to have a true love in real life in order to break the curse. . . . I don't think anyone's ever tried kissing a person here in Diamant."

Snow White thought for a moment. The idea of it was slightly embarrassing . . . to go home, save her kingdom with just one kiss? No more trials, no more traveling, no more danger. Just a simple kiss and it could all be over. Surely she could find a way to save the others in Diamant once she was awake, once she defeated the Queen.

She forced herself to look at him then, suddenly noticing things about him she never had before. The way his eyes reflected the embers, glinting amber through the brown—like the tigereye stone. The way his reassuring smile gave him a little dimple in his cheek. He looked rather sweet when he wasn't scowling.

"We could try," she said.

Henry nodded and closed his eyes.

Snow White closed hers, too. But she suddenly wasn't picturing grumpy, gallant Henry—she was picturing a bandit with bright, mischievous eyes. And all at once, the truth weighed on her.

This was never going to work.

"I'm sorry, Henry," she said, moving away. "I can't."

"It's okay," he said, his eyes reassuring her that it truly was.

"I've grown so fond of you over this journey, I really have," said Snow White. "But what I feel for you, it's not true love. A kiss won't save us if the feelings aren't true."

Henry leaned back against the wall with a sigh. "I'm not even sure why I thought it would ever work. Don't get me wrong—I care about you. It feels a little like some sort of love. It's just not . . . you know . . ."

"I know. I'm not offended," she said with a small laugh. "We can't force what's not there. Besides, platonic love is just as wonderful."

"It's too bad platonic love can't get us home." He seemed just as relieved as she was that true love wasn't an option for them. After all, true love wasn't something that could be forced.

"So, who is he?" Henry asked.

Snow White blinked at him; it was such an odd subject change. "Who is who?"

"The prince you love. What kingdom is he from?"

Snow White scowled. "Why does there have to be a prince in the picture just because I'm a princess?"

He shrugged. "Aren't you supposed to marry a prince?"

"I think a princess can marry whomever she likes. Or not marry at all, if that's what she prefers. She can live by her own rules."

Henry smiled. "Fair enough."

"And what about you?" she asked, giving him a teasing poke in the arm. "Who did you leave heartbroken back at home?"

Henry chuckled, folding his arms across his chest. "My father was arranging a marriage for me with the baker's daughter before all this happened. We got along, and I liked her. I could have grown to love her, maybe, if we'd had more time. . . ." He shrugged. "That's the extent of my romantic life, I'm afraid . . . the extent of my social life, really. I'd always been more concerned with learning my craft."

"There's nothing wrong with that, either. Sometimes"— Snow White felt herself blushing as her mind drifted to Jonathan—"love can strike you when you least expect it."

Love . . . it wasn't love she was feeling for Jonathan, was it? For a thief she had helped escape from the dungeon. The same thief who had helped save her from her own soldiers. The one she felt so good and safe with . . . She certainly cared for him and enjoyed his company. But love . . . ?

Yes. Maybe it was. Otherwise, why would she have such a strange, warm feeling just thinking about him? A feeling she'd never had for anyone else.

She blinked and snapped herself out of her thoughts, and when she looked at Henry, he was grinning.

"So, who is he?" he asked again.

Snow White laughed. "You really want to know, don't you?"

"All I'm saying is that you were blushing pretty hard a moment ago, and that couldn't have been over nothing."

"I could not have been blushing *that* hard." Snow White covered her warm cheeks with her hands. It was true; there was no sense in denying it now—not when Henry had seen the proof of her affection right on her face. And besides, it would be nice to be open and honest with a true friend. "Well, if you must know . . . there is someone. And he's nothing close to a prince."

The wider Henry's grin became, the more Snow White blushed. "You're excited about this one, huh?"

"Oh, Henry!" Snow White blurted, unable to hold it in any longer. "Have you ever met someone who just understands you? Who allows you to be you and makes you feel so good while doing it?"

Henry shook his head, and Snow White took hold of his hands tightly.

"It's such a wonderful feeling," she said. "And I want that for you someday. I know when you aren't even looking for it, you'll find it."

"If you say so, I'm inclined to believe you." Henry smiled. "But I already have plenty of love in my life," he said, touching the pearls around his neck, and it made Snow White's heart sing. "I have a true friend, thanks to you, and my sister. And soon . . . *hopefully* soon, we'll find the Ruby Heart. And then I'll have my father back, too. I really do have all the love I need at the moment."

"What about the baker's daughter?"

Henry sighed. "It's been five years. I hope by now my father gave up on the idea and she moved on with her life. She's a sweet person, and I wish her the best. It would be nice to think she met someone the way you did. Fell in love and all that."

"That's so wonderful that you think that way, Henry. We'll make an optimist out of you before the night is over."

They laughed and then simply sat together for a

moment, listening to the rain and enjoying the warmth of the coals with love in their hearts.

"Perhaps we should get some sleep for tomorrow," said Snow White.

"For tomorrow, when we're still stuck in this cave?"

Snow White shook her head at her friend. "Henry."

"You are *not* going to make an optimist out of me. Besides, are you even tired?"

"Not really."

"Then I was thinking," Henry said, "since it's obvious a kiss won't work, we might as well press forward with the map."

Snow White sat up from the wall to look at him. "Shouldn't we wait for Mouse?"

"It's going to take some time. . . . Do you want to wait that long?"

Snow White scrunched her nose in distaste and shook her head. "What's the map say?"

She was relieved Henry had gone back to believing in the map, in their mission. They needed each other—she was sure of it—to finish what they had started. And since both of them seemed to be recovered from their ordeal with the river, there was no better time than the present to begin. They couldn't wait for Mouse to come back with others;

that much was clear. No, they needed to get to the Ruby Heart and finish this. The lives of so many depended on it.

Henry held up the map between them. The coals delivered more warmth than light, so it was difficult to see the details of the map save for the glowing path . . . and the word *Brave* written where they had just been. On the bridge.

"So the bridge *was* one of the trials," murmured Henry. "Or perhaps the river?"

"Perhaps both," said Snow White. "The box at the end of the bridge triggered it all, I think. The rockslide didn't happen until I opened the box and it caused a vibration through the stone wall."

"That makes sense now. I didn't notice anything natural that could have caused it. That's two trials down, then. One to go."

"Look, Henry," said Snow White, running her finger along a glowing line on the parchment. "The map is showing us the way to the final trial."

And indeed, the glowing path continued on . . . into the depths of the cavern they were at the mouth of at that very moment. But the path went into the cavern and disappeared, as if the glowing light on the map was literally traveling through a dark cave and couldn't sustain itself in there.

Whether the cavern was haunted or not, they were headed in the right direction.

Henry eyed the path warily. "I am most definitely not looking forward to this."

Snow White smirked. "I promise to protect you from the ghosts."

"You scoff now. Just wait."

The rain stopped abruptly, and the clouds swiftly shifted, unveiling the full moon. The light was bright, with some jewels reflecting it more than others, creating a glowing path through the cavernous tunnel.

"What do you think, Princess?" Henry got to his feet before waiting for an answer. "This path looks bright enough to navigate."

"More than bright enough." Snow White dusted off her skirt as she joined him. "And it's *Stardrop* to you, thank you very much."

Henry grinned, and they headed into the depths of the cavern.

The tunnel was unlike anything Snow White had ever seen. The jewels embedded in the walls, ceilings, and floor of the cave shone bright like stars in a night sky, glowing as if the light came from within them. As if they were bioluminescent plants, except all of it seemed far less natural and much more . . . magical. Even farther into the tunnel the lights still guided them—each gem catching the reflections of the moonlight from the ones before it and passing the magic along.

Henry held on to Snow White's shoulder with one hand while Snow White slid her hand over the wall to help guide them through the dim tunnel. There was no way they were going to let anything separate them, like the bridge and wild rapids had. Nor would they let a trap surprise them this time. They were prepared for whatever the Queen had to throw at them. And Snow White knew that because they were so close to the Ruby Heart, the Queen was going throw everything she had.

Still, these lights didn't seem full of dread and foreboding. Not necessarily good magic, because even wicked things could be beautiful. The Queen herself was a perfect example of that.

"I think," whispered Snow White, her voice reverberating the slightest bit against the shimmering walls without any effort on her part, "this cavern must be the most beautiful place in Diamant."

"Yes," murmured Henry, looking around carefully. "Before, of course, it tries to kill us."

Such a horrifying thought, even if it was necessary to consider it.

They walked on for a bit more before Henry pulled Snow White to a stop.

"Did you hear that?" he asked, glancing around the tunnel quickly with his hand on the hilt of his sword.

Snow White listened, but after the echo of Henry's voice had vanished, there was nothing left to hear. She

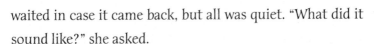

waited in case it came back, but all was quiet. "What did it sound like?" she asked.

"A squeaking sound," he said, "like a rusty hinge, or—" He froze, then drew his sword. "There it was again. You must have heard it this time."

She had been actively listening that time, and still she had to shake her head, even if a part of her was beginning to feel a little paranoid. "Let's just keep moving. And be on our guard."

They walked on, perhaps a bit more quickly now. The sound had most definitely been something; Henry wasn't just hearing things out of anticipation. A trap was coming, Snow White knew. And more than anything, she wanted to be ready for it. Because getting through the trap would mean they were that much closer to the Ruby Heart.

And then Snow White halted quickly so her footsteps wouldn't conceal what she was hearing. There *was* a squeaking sound . . . and something about it was familiar.

"There," Henry murmured when the sound arose again. "What is that?"

"It's . . ." Snow White finally recognized it when she heard it again. No, it couldn't be. . . . "A mouse?"

The squeaking continued, but this time there was more than one source. More and more mice squeaking, louder and louder, the walls of the tunnel echoing the sounds eerily. And soon, in addition to the terrifying squeaking, they could hear the scratching of dozens and dozens of small-clawed feet scampering across the stone ground. The sound raced closer, far too quickly for Snow White to decide what to do.

They both stood frozen, falling silent as small glowing eyes peered at them through the darkness. They glowed green as emeralds, but unlike the leaves on the trees, they were a sinister hue. They were hostile glares, to be sure. The Queen's creatures.

"We should run," Henry whispered.

But as the mice moved closer, Snow White saw the pairs of eyes multiply. There had to have been at least fifty creatures, quickly growing to one hundred, as if they were spawning from the walls or the floor or each other. They were running with a purpose, but Snow White was no longer afraid of any living creatures in this cruel world the Queen had created. What the Queen saw as something that could frighten, deter, or even defeat her, Snow White saw as the best way to display her strength.

And she was determined to show it once again.

The mice abruptly stopped three feet in front of them and stared . . . simply stared. Because the squeaking had stopped, all Snow White heard was her friend's nervous breaths.

"Henry," Snow White said quietly, carefully, doing her best not to startle the creatures, "put your sword away."

"That's a bad idea," he said, staring at the hundreds of pairs of eyes staring back him, unwavering.

"You're going to want to fight them—"

"Rightfully so."

"And we both know that's not how this works." Snow White nodded at him, hoping he could see her reassuring look in the dimness. "Please, Henry."

Henry hesitated for a moment. "I hope you know what you're doing," And then slowly, reluctantly, he sheathed his sword.

And that was when the mice attacked.

Snow White and Henry barely had time to cover their faces with their arms before the mice raced up their bodies. Their tiny emerald claws scratched at their clothing, their arms, and Snow White suddenly thought that perhaps Henry had had the right idea in running, after all. They swiped at the creatures with their hands, but every time they managed to knock one away, another took its place, and soon she felt herself being forced to her knees from the sheer weight of the vicious bodies all over her.

Soon Snow White felt suffocated, and she fought the creatures from pushing her all the way down to the ground. If she lost more leverage than she already had, there was no way she would be able to get up again.

It would be over.

"No!" Snow White shouted, igniting adrenaline in her body to go on. "This is not the end!"

But she was only human, and the weight of the creatures was heavy indeed.

"Take my hands!" Henry said. Snow White managed to lift her arms to take them, and he pulled her to her feet. She had to kick off from the ground to do it, and when she did, she scared three mice, which ran off into the darkness.

She watched the mice run. So quick movements scared them. And suddenly, she knew what to do.

"Henry!" Snow White called. "Remember the dance we did during the party?"

"Please tell me there's a good reason you're asking that!" he shouted back desperately.

"Dance with me."

Henry looked at Snow White, his eyes sparking with understanding.

And they started the dance . . . slowly at first, as the

mice weighed down their limbs. But as they flung their arms and kicked up their legs, more mice went running. Soon they picked up momentum, kicking and turning to the memory of the music. The more they were able to move, the quicker their dance became. Arms thrown up, spin, kick! The distressed squeaks of the mice grew softer and softer as they ran off down the tunnel.

Snow White and Henry danced and danced, and soon they were laughing, their bodies no longer weighed down, as the last of the mice retreated into the darkness of the cavern, from whence they had come.

They spun one final time and gave each other a victorious hug.

"We did it!" Snow White cried.

"I can't believe that worked," said Henry, and then he chuckled. "I need to stop saying that. *Of course* it worked!"

They parted, holding each other at arm's length, and paused to listen. There were no squeaks to be heard, not even echoing in the distance. No scratches of tiny wicked claws against the walls and ground. No sinister glowing eyes.

They had done it.

"We did it," Snow White repeated, stepping away from

Henry to look around, smiling. "You truly are the best dancer in all of Diamant."

Henry grinned. "It helps when I have a genius of a partner."

Snow White let out a breath in relief. She took Henry's hand and led him along the path again. It was better to keep moving. If the mice tried to come back, moving was the only way to get rid of them again.

Eventually the reflective gems changed pattern, from twinkling strings to upside-down Vs. Much like the sign that had been left at the entrance, there was an unnatural-ness about them, as if they had been purposefully placed that way.

Then, suddenly, there was a blinding light, reflected by the gems. Ahead, the moonlight shone bright at the end of the tunnel, filling the space.

"That's it," said Henry. "We're almost there."

Henry's excitement was contagious, and they ran. Ran toward the light, toward the openness, toward the—

Snow White tripped, as if the floor had shifted beneath her feet, and Henry caught her before she could fall into one of the walls. There was a screech, like the cry of a banshee, a horrifying sound that echoed from down the tunnel they had just come from. It chilled Snow White to her bones.

"This could be another trap," Snow White said, regaining her footing.

The screech rang out again, closer this time.

Henry looked around warily. "I don't think we should linger to find out."

They rushed forward toward the light but were quickly thrown off-balance by an intense rumble.

"We can't run from this, Henry," Snow White said. "The only way to get through this trap is to face it, the same as the others."

Henry looked into the darkness of the tunnel. "Face what, is the part that worries me."

Usually, Snow White would counter Henry's concern with hope and boundless determination, but in this particular moment his worry seemed justified. Still, the Queen had only gemstones at her disposal. Snow White thought back to the traps that hadn't involved wild creatures. The first trap had come from the sky—those gem leaves falling from the trees. The second, from the ground—that crawling crystal that had tried to consume Henry. This time, Snow White was sure it would involve the walls.

Well . . . 80 percent sure.

"Let's not touch the walls," she said. "I think the trap will come from there."

Henry glanced at the glowing walls. "Do you think the trap will involve spikes?"

"We should be ready for anything."

"On second thought," said Henry, analyzing the walls, "we can probably rule out spikes. Those would only be a danger to us if the walls—"

The screeching echoed down the tunnel and was followed by a rumble like the growl of a massive beast. Both Snow White and Henry were frozen, watching the tunnel, ready to take on whatever trap the Queen had for them.

If only they knew what that trap would be.

And then there was a horrible abrasive sound, like stone scraping on stone, cracking, crumbling. Snow White cringed, covering her head with her arms as the rumbling jolted a rain of dust on top of them. She coughed, waving the dust from her view so she could see what was moving up ahead. Because there *was* something moving ahead. . . .

"What is that?" Henry muttered, gripping the hilt of his sword but also rocking on his feet, unsure of what the trap required of him: fight or flight.

It wasn't a creature pursuing them or spikes shooting from the walls. They watched as the glowing stones at the end of the tunnel disappeared . . . and began dimming and dying closer and closer . . . and closer—until Snow White

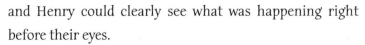
and Henry could clearly see what was happening right before their eyes.

The walls ahead were slamming in on each other, one segment at a time.

Snow White's heart dropped into her feet. "I changed my mind, Henry. I think we should probably run."

Henry didn't ask any questions. The two of them simply turned and ran.

Faster and faster the walls collapsed behind them, like thick, giant doors, shaking the ground and ceiling. Chasing, as if they were something alive, while Snow White and Henry fought to run and stay on their feet despite the constant rumbling. The exit of the cavern was so close.

But Snow White's pulse picked up when the gems began to rain down—not on her and Henry, but near the opening. Larger stones fell as the ceiling cracked and crumbled. All too quickly, the piling rocks began blocking the light of the moon. The ceiling was caving in.

But neither captivity nor death was an option for the two companions—not when they were so close to the Ruby Heart.

"We're not going to make it!" shouted Henry.

"We have to!" Snow White shouted back.

But the walls were closing in to meet the tumbling

stones, and Snow White was beginning to think that perhaps it would take a miracle for the two of them to reach the exit in time.

Because suddenly there was barely any moonlight left to light the way ahead of them, and the collapsing walls were right on their tail. If either of them tripped, it would all be over. Both obstructions were rapidly drawing closer to crushing Snow White and Henry.

She reached a point where she could deny it no longer. *It's over, Snow White*, she thought, sensing the inevitable. *This is the end.*

There was no other option. Preparing to be crushed together, they wrapped their arms around each other and dropped to the ground.

As soon as the two of them hit the ground, the walls halted and the final stone fell.

Immediately, the cavern was swallowed by a deep darkness; with no more moonlight flowing through, the gems had no light to catch and reflect. Everything all around them was silent save for the last few tumbles of small stones and one final rumble through the earth, like a massive monster swallowing its prey.

The air was thin now; everything fresh and good from

the outdoors was completely shut out. But at the same time, it was thick with dirt and dust. The two of them managed to get to their hands and knees, coughing and waving the dust away from their faces.

"Are you all right?" Snow White heard Henry ask. It was a desperate question. His voice sounded right beside her, yet she couldn't even make out the outline of his form in the dark. She touched his shoulder, to make sure his voice had not been just a trick of her ear.

"I'm all right," she replied, relieved he was alive, but also thankful he couldn't see her wince. Her knee was throbbing and burning—she had probably skinned it when she fell—but other than that she was just fine.

Physically, anyway.

Inside, her heart was pounding with frustration. Before they had entered the tunnel, she had known to expect a trap, yet it had turned out to be as unpredictable as the traps before it. The only thing she was certain of was that they were close to the final trial. They had to be, or else the Queen wouldn't have gotten so desperate. She knew she was about to lose.

"Well," Henry muttered, "you were right about the walls."

Snow White heard a scratching sound and saw the flash of an orange glow as Henry brought a small coal to life with his flint. He held it on the flat of his sword so they could carry it while looking over the damage the cave-in had caused. The sight of the two walls behind them pressing together as if they were one emphasized the gravity of what would have happened if they had not gotten away from them in time. And in front of them was nothing but rocks filling up the height of the cavern.

They couldn't move forward with their way blocked by a pile of rocks. They couldn't go back through the cavern to where they had come from and find another way. The trap the Queen had laid had done its work. They were, indeed, trapped in the small space—and with very few options.

"Maybe we could dig our way out of here," said Snow White, looking at the piled stones.

"That is one option," Henry said, leaning against a wall with a sigh. "Realistically, we could. The problem is that the only tool we have is my sword, and I wouldn't doubt if it took an entire day or more. I'd prefer an easier way, if we can find one." He fished out the map and unfolded it, but the path didn't so much as spark in any direction. The map couldn't see a path any more than they could.

"We have to think about this, Henry," said Snow White,

leaning on the opposite wall to face him. "There has to be something we're overlooking."

"Something we're overlooking?" Henry murmured. He thought for a moment. "All the trials and traps have been catered to your skills and thought processes. The way out of here isn't the way that would be the most obvious."

"That's sweet of you to say, Henry"—she paused and blinked at him—"I think."

"Well, it's true. We can't go back, and trying to dig ourselves out will take forever." He paced for a moment in the small space. "Which means you're right: we must be over—"

"Overlooking something!" Snow White said at the same time Henry did, looking up at the ceiling just as he did. Their eyes were wide with discovery.

A gamble, maybe. But they were running out of options. And air.

Besides, if the map didn't see a path, the only logical conclusion was that they had to make their own.

"Do you think that perhaps those strangely arranged gems from earlier were trying to tell us something?" Snow White said, her excited voice echoing in the small space. "They were pointing upward. Perhaps they were a sign that the only way out is through the ceiling."

"All right. Watch out," Henry said, holding out a hand

to Snow White, directing her to stay against the wall. "Cover your face. I'm going to try something."

When Snow White was ready, Henry thrust his sword into the ceiling, the diamond blade penetrating the stone easily. When he pulled it out, a few rocks rained down with it, but something more glorious did, too.

Light.

Henry exclaimed, making Snow White open her eyes. Then she was screaming, too, and their voices bounced off the cavern walls.

The diamond of Henry's sword had pieced clean through whatever stone the cave was made of, revealing the surface above. It provided space for only a thin sliver of moonlight to shine through, but it was enough light to activate the gems around them, making them glow and illuminate the small area they were contained in.

"Henry!" Snow White exclaimed, grabbing on to his arm and shaking him.

"I know!" he replied.

"What are you waiting for? Keep stabbing it."

Henry shook his head and smirked at her. "That sounds violent, Stardrop. What's gotten into you?"

Snow White laughed. "We're almost there, that's what! Now demolish that ceiling, Henry."

Henry took the command seriously. He stabbed and slashed and dug into the rocky ceiling until it fell away. Because the blade was sharp and solid, it didn't take too much effort, and soon he'd made a hole wide enough for a person to fit through. He finished it off by thrusting the sword upward one last time, and then the two of them stood beneath the hole, bathed in moonlight.

Snow White leapt at Henry and hugged him tightly. "You did it!"

"Only because I thought like you," said Henry. He beamed at her. "Does this change your mind about swords?"

Snow White chuckled. "Not even a little."

Henry raised a brow at her as he knelt down and laced his fingers together near the ground, offering his hands to her as a platform. "Princesses first."

Snow White laid her hand on his shoulder, placing her foot in his hands. "I thought there were no special exceptions made for princesses."

"Oh, did I not mention? In the event of friendship, the rule is void."

Snow White grinned at him, her heart swelling as the pearls around his neck shimmered in the light. And then she allowed him to boost her up through the hole, into the open air.

She grabbed hold of the side of the hole and pulled herself up and out of it, only truly taking in her surroundings when she was on her feet.

Snow White stood on a hill, which sloped down to meet a field. Except it was nothing like the field where they had encountered the wolves. That one had been healthy, green, and overgrown, whereas this one was filled with a wide stretch of gravel, like a field of crops long dead. There were no animals, no water, nothing to block the horizon. The sky above it was full of impending doom—deadly dark, like an abyss, not a star or cloud breaking its mood . . . nothing but the enormous full moon, like a looming eye watching Snow White's and Henry's every move, casting a ghostly light against all the jewels. And at the center of the clearing stood a tree.

It was large and as ominous-looking as the sky. Made of pure onyx that reflected as slick as oil in the moonlight. Wild leafless branches hatched the moon with sharp marks, like a thicket of thorns threatening anyone who approached. It dripped dark sap from the trunk, from the branches. And in its trunk was a hollow, like a gaping mouth.

It was foreboding. Sinister . . . terrifying.

"This can't be right," Henry murmured, as he often did,

stepping up beside her. But this time Snow White had to agree with him.

Because as they walked cautiously down the steep slope and made their way closer to the tree, the more convinced Snow White became that its harsh bark was leaking blood, thick and sap-like. Inside the tree, in the shallow hollow in the trunk, sat something red and glowing . . . pulsing. Like a—

"The Ruby Heart," gasped Snow White.

Henry opened his mouth to speak when there was a flash—bright as lightning—of moonlight off glass. The two of them shielded their eyes, blinking away stars from the fierceness of it. And suddenly, instead of the Ruby·Heart, there was a full-length mirror embedded in the trunk of the tree, as if it had always been there. The frame was made of the intricately carved onyx of the trunk, with the word *True*, glowing like a fresh wound, carved into the top.

Henry fished out the map, and sure enough, the word *True* glowed on the page. This was it: the final trial.

In addition to the strangeness of the mirror's arrival, Snow White noted that it looked very much like the type of mirror she grew up seeing at home. Perhaps it wasn't a trick. She took a deep, determined breath and started moving toward the mirror, but Henry held her back.

"You can't be serious," he said, and she had to admit he was right. It was much better to be cautious; the tree looked like it would awaken and start swinging its thorny branches at them at any second.

"All right, I won't touch it. But we have to figure this out or we'll never get around this mirror," she said. " 'True,' " she read. "What does a mirror have to do with truth?"

"What you look like? Like a reflection?"

"Maybe." She chewed on her lip. She thought back to the previous trials. What did they all have in common?

One thing was that the trial wouldn't begin until they leapt into it with both feet.

"Then again," said Henry, "looking at our reflections seems too simple to be the answer."

"Well, we have to touch it," Snow White replied. "Or look into it. I don't know which. All I know is the wolves didn't surround us until we entered the field, and the rocks didn't start falling until I crossed the bridge. It's clear we have to do something to initiate the trial."

"Yes!" Henry lit up. "And all the words meant something for the other trials. Fair, brave . . . true. It could be the two of us expressing the truth to each other."

"But it's a mirror," Snow White said, studying it. "Perhaps . . . we have to express the truth to ourselves."

Henry huffed in frustration. "But what does that even mean?"

They heard a small familiar voice, as thin and treacherous as a ghost: "I know what it means."

Snow White and Henry both turned to look at once. Mouse stood at the entrance of the cavern—or where the entrance would have been if it hadn't been blocked by the fallen rocks. There was no way she could have exited through there, no way she could have followed them. There must have been another way here, one that wasn't shown on the map.

There must have been . . . because the alternative—that Mouse had just appeared out of thin air—was far too odd to entertain.

"You were supposed to be going for help," Henry said accusingly, his voice hard.

It was difficult to tell from a distance, but Mouse seemed to smile. "If I had done that, I would have missed all the fun."

Snow White felt the prickle of goose bumps rising on her arms. She touched Henry's hand to reassure him before approaching the little girl.

The walk seemed quiet . . . ominous. As if the very air around her had paused to observe.

"Mouse," Snow White said to break that wicked silence. "If you know what the word on the mirror means, you should tell us."

Mouse didn't respond.

As Snow White got closer, she could see the gleam in the girl's eyes, a look that clearly said she knew something they didn't.

But before she could say anything more, Mouse shouted, "Can't catch me!" and took off running toward her.

Snow White braced to grab the girl, but she ran past her. She was surprisingly fast. "Mouse!" Snow White called as she turned and chased after her. "What are you doing?"

But the little girl didn't listen. Instead, she ran at full speed toward Henry. Toward the tree. Toward the mirror.

"Mouse!" Snow White's voice rose with alarm.

It didn't look like Mouse was going to stop. Henry lunged to grab her, but she dodged under his arm. She was going to slam directly into—

The glass of the mirror rippled like water as Mouse leapt through it, disappearing.

Snow White and Henry tripped to a stop, looking at each other. Dread filled Snow White's gut. There was something

very wrong, and their answers somehow lay in the mirror—
with Mouse. Snow White turned her attention back to the
mirror. The surface of it still rippled like a dark, disturbed
lake. Snow White didn't know where it would lead them,
but one thing was clear: the final trial had begun.

She and Henry each took a deep breath and then
charged into the dark surface of the mirror together.

11

"Mouse?"

Snow White was sure she was awake, with her eyes wide open. She even blinked a few times to be certain. Yet she could hardly see a thing; even when she lifted her own hand in front of her face, part of her wasn't entirely sure it was there. Darkness swirled around her, a fog that threatened to suffocate her with its nearness. And the stench that wafted off the fog was . . . cold. Not like wintertime. It wasn't nearly natural enough for that. More like the chill of a steel blade, of sadness and loneliness.

Of wicked magic.

"Mouse," she tried again, firmly. "Where are you?"

For a second, there was no response. A second . . . even though she had no idea how much time had passed. Time, space, and reality seemed to swirl around her just as slowly as the darkness, erasing all rhyme and reason.

Then, suddenly, Henry's voice rang out: "Snow White!" And she saw that he was standing only a few feet in front of her, tangled in the swirling of the fog. But when she reached for him, he disappeared within it again, and she couldn't feel a thing, even though she would have sworn his body had been only a few feet away.

Her heart pounded as she tried to walk to where she had just seen him, her arms outstretched in front of her, but the fog was too disorienting. And perhaps she had walked the wrong way—or he had been trying to get to her, too—because she saw his hand reach out from somewhere beside her instead of in front. But when she tried to grab his hand, he was gone again.

The two of them tried desperately to get to each other, but every time they tried, the fog shifted, like a monster with a life of its own. For a while it taunted them with glimpses of each other, until Snow White's heart was pounding, until finally they couldn't see or hear each other at all.

And maybe it *was* a monster, because something sharp

suddenly slid past Snow White's arm. She yelped and grabbed her wound, panicked to feel her arm throbbing, her fingers coming away wet with warm blood. Something caught her skirt, her sleeve, trying to cut her but being blocked by the thick fabric.

"Henry?" Snow White called, if only for comfort. But the sound of her voice was muted, static, traveling nowhere but to her own ears. "Henry!" She tried again, but the cry never left her throat. She grabbed her neck, frightened by the lack of control she had over her own voice, her own volume. Was it her voice leaving her or was it the fog?

Or was it . . . something else?

Snow White took a deep breath. "Is this your final trial?" she said to the Queen, who she knew might be listening. "If this is all you have for me, it's not nearly enough to destroy my spirit."

She stood there for a moment in a consuming silence, broken only by her trembling breath. The silence and the cold. It was more than just steel and loneliness. It was deeply penetrating her bones. It was hopelessness.

She couldn't give in to that. She couldn't let hopelessness overtake her mind.

There were too many people depending on her.

"I am not afraid of you," she said as she looked around

slowly, attempting to find an opening in the fog. "Are you afraid of me?"

The Queen must have taken the accusatory question personally, because the fog suddenly dropped to the ground and skimmed around her feet, revealing large shards of mirror that slowly floated in the air. That was what had cut her, clearly, and she was thankful her injury had not been worse. She let out a breath of relief when she saw that Henry was no more than a few feet away from her. He had a thin, raw cut on his cheek and one on his arm. Relief flooded his expression, too, when they locked eyes, but anger overshadowed it as he unsheathed his sword.

Unfortunately, Snow White had a feeling swords would be of no use here, as in the other trials.

She touched the flat surface of one of the glass shards to redirect it from hitting her in the face, and it switched direction as if weightless. The two of them warily watched it float away, but now was not the time to get distracted. Henry tapped more shards near them with his sword to send them away, but when Snow White stepped toward Henry through the path he had cleared, the mirror shards moved to block her way, as if they had a mind of their own.

There was no sense in trying again. From the swirling

fog and the razor-edged mirrors, it was clear that whatever trial she was about to master, she'd have to do it alone.

However, Henry was fuming.

"What is this place?" he demanded of no one—because it seemed no one was there to answer.

But someone was. Before them, in the eye of the swirling vortex of dirty fog, stood Mouse.

The shards reflected things, but not anything present in the fog. They showed Mouse on their surfaces, to be sure, but not as Snow White saw the girl now. It was as if a scene was taking place, a moment was playing out in front of them, but only in the world within the glass. The Mouse in the glass was sitting on a bed made of wood with a real mattress, playing with a doll—a doll that was suddenly stolen away from her by a faceless person. *Memories*, thought Snow White. That was what they were seeing.

Then the shards shifted again, and in them Mouse was sitting at a real wooden table—in a home made of bricks instead of gemstones—with an unfinished plate of food before her; she watched forlornly as other little girls played outside.

The shards moved around Mouse, and dread filled Snow White's stomach as one passed by the little girl's face and reflected a face that wasn't hers. Or perhaps it was hers, but older—with the same brown eyes and dark hair. It now held the vicious-sweet expression Snow White had seen for half her life.

It was the face of the Queen.

Mouse's eyes glowed unnaturally, as wicked as they had been in Snow White's nightmare the first night and as ruthless as in her hallucination in the river. They were eyes that could mean nothing but ill to anyone they gazed upon, even set in the little girl's face. Snow White hadn't seen it at first, but now the resemblance could not be denied.

And now it all made perfect sense. Tabitha had told her the Queen had created Diamant when she was very young and just beginning to learn her magic. Perhaps Mouse had been there before anyone else because she *was* the Queen, or at least a part of her subconscious that remained there— placed to guard over the world she had created, to ensure no one left.

"Did you really think I'd let you take my Ruby Heart so easily?" Mouse said darkly, the shards around her echoing her words in the voice of a grown woman. "You, Snow White, of all people?"

She let out a wicked laugh as she lifted her small hands, with her adult reflections mirroring her, and commanded the shards to fly at Snow White and Henry. Snow White lifted her arms to block them. But as Mouse—the Queen—vanished, her maniacal laughter becoming nothing but an echo, the shards stopped around them as they had around her.

Snow White covered her mouth with her hand. She was startled, stunned as she watched . . . herself. In the reflections, she was on the ground, waking up beside Henry near the sinister hollow tree.

I don't remember this, she thought. *This can't be my past. . . .*

Snow White blinked, and in the next moment she saw both herself and Henry on horseback, galloping toward a village she had never seen before. The scene dissipated like smoke, and now she saw a multitude of farmers and shop owners, men and women alike preparing supplies for travel, donning their armor, saddling horses. Henry, working at a forge, focused as he crafted a new sword and armor of the most beautiful golden hue—and in the next moment Snow White saw herself putting that armor on, and it was the perfect fit.

In the next instant the scene shifted again. A massive army, in full armor and holding weapons, charged forward on horseback, with her and Henry leading them. They looked as fierce as lions against the pink and orange light of a sunrise glaring like a beacon against their already shining armor, casting them in a radiant golden glow.

And the Queen stood at her window, brown eyes not so arrogant anymore as she shook with fear.

Snow White squeezed her eyes shut. What *was* this? She'd stood near the tree but had never touched the Ruby Heart. The town clearly wasn't Diamant, because it was made of more than just stone and she didn't recognize anyone; Tabitha hadn't even been there. And she had never worn armor in her life. No, this wasn't her past. So was it possible she was seeing . . . her future?

Or what *could* be the future if she would just kiss Henry with true love in her heart so they could go home.

It was a violent option; a battle was more violence than she would ever be comfortable with. And she loved Henry dearly, but it was not the kind of love that could send them home. How could that be her future? It couldn't be. Nothing about it seemed right.

She opened her eyes and gasped, because the scene changed and there was Jonathan looking at her from within the glass. Brave, charming Jonathan. Most would call him an unworthy thief, but he was her heart. In the scene displayed on the shards, he knelt on the ground over her and kissed her so sweetly it woke her from this nightmare of a place. And together, she and Jonathan and her friends went back to her kingdom and—

Yes. That one. She didn't have to consider. It was that one. Maybe both scenarios were true—*could* be true, but that was up to her, wasn't it? She could choose her truth.

And her truth didn't need to be vile, didn't need to sink to the Queen's level, to be effective. She did not need to start a war to save her kingdom from the horrors of the Queen. All she had to do was be like her father—fair, brave . . . true.

And with that, Snow White took a deep breath.

And closed her eyes.

S now White jolted awake, as if she'd been dropped from a great height. She winced, panting at the sky—but not the void that had been inside the mirror a moment earlier. There were no glass shards floating around her or cruel, consuming fog, only a light breeze and the stars overhead. She was looking at the *actual* sky—not the vicious version of it, but simply the normal shades of night.

Did we do it? she wondered.

Wait, we? "Henry!" she called, looking around quickly, her heart sprinting. But a hand grabbed hers before she could sit up. Seeing Henry beside her, she released a breath in relief and moved closer to him. They lay on the ground as they had done the night they danced, except this time the two of them were not full of laughter and joy. Tonight they held on as if they would break if they let go. They looked at each other, and in Henry's eyes Snow White saw what she felt: Fear. Awe. Purpose.

But above all that, certainty.

"Are you okay?" he asked.

Snow White nodded as she frowned at his injury and touched the cut on his cheek with her fingers ever so gently. There was no denying what had just happened was real, not when the proof of it was right there on Henry's slashed face. "Are you?"

"It doesn't hurt," he assured her.

She looked up and saw that they were indeed lying beside the tree. It was still as black as ink, and its branches stabbed toward the sky like a thicket of thorns. But from there, the story deviated. Because just as the sky had recovered from the Queen's wicked possession, so had the tree. It held no more power; it was just a tree made of stone, no longer full of malice. The sap it had been bleeding had dried up, and the center of its trunk was whole, as if the hollow had never been. It looked more sad than wicked now, like something dead and decaying but still upright because nothing had come by to knock it over. This was indeed different from her vision. Nothing there could hurt them anymore; Snow White was sure of it.

"I saw things," Henry gasped suddenly, stealing her from her thoughts.

"So did I," she replied quietly.

"The mirror showed me my future"—he hesitated, staring at their hands linked, gripping each other like a lifeline—"*our* future."

Snow White's heart dropped. So Henry had seen the same things she had—and perhaps he had chosen the future she had not. But how could he have, if that was not the future she had chosen for herself?

She pushed on the ground to sit up. At their feet, the mirror was gone. In its place lay the open map. Below *True*, there was now the image of the Ruby Heart. Snow White's heart leapt. They had done it.

They had actually done it.

She took the map in both hands, and when she looked up again she saw the Ruby Heart lying at the roots of the tree. Henry sat up as well, and together they stared at it, unsure of what to do next.

"That really is the Ruby Heart," Henry murmured. "We really did it. . . ."

Still in awe of what they had just accomplished, Henry

didn't move, so Snow White put the map aside, reached over, and carefully picked up the Ruby Heart with both hands.

It was made of pure ruby, deep red in color and solid to the touch. Yet there was something *alive* about it. Much like the wolves and the crows and the mice, the Ruby Heart was an uncanny being, something that should not have been able to exist in any world. She watched as its chambers pumped, its veins and arteries shimmering with dark movement as if it belonged in someone's chest. Whose chest, she didn't know.

The idea was unsettling, to say the least.

"What do we do now?" Snow White asked.

Henry shook his head, his expression disbelieving. "I'd always hoped, but . . . I never really thought we'd get this far. I've never actually thought of what we'd do with the heart once we found it."

"Well, how does it work, exactly? Is it the same as the Wishing Grain?" The Ruby Heart pulsed against her, but if she thought of it as a cocoon containing a butterfly about to burst free, the steady rhythm was actually quite lovely. "Do the legends say anything about that?"

Henry shrugged. "You have to touch it while you make a wish on it. That's all I know."

"We came all the way here . . . but I never thought to question whether or not the Ruby Heart *could* send everyone in Diamant home until now." She looked at Henry. "If I touch it and wish, will that be enough?"

"I'm not sure," Henry said solemnly. "But if it's like the Wishing Grain, once you spend your wish, it will crumble away into dust. So we really only have one chance at this."

One use. One wish. And most likely only one of them would get to wish it, without a guarantee that anyone else could benefit from the wish.

But then again . . .

A minute earlier, she had thought that the heart held a power she desperately needed. That it was the only way she would ever get home to save her kingdom. But . . . someone *loved* her. She could wake up with true love's kiss, Ruby Heart or not.

"You take it," she said, holding it out to Henry.

He gaped at her. "You're too selfless for your own good, you know that?" He moved her hands back toward her and shook his head. "I've been here in Diamant so long that I have . . . well, judging by what I saw in those mirror shards, I have nothing to go back to. But I have my sister here. I have someone, something, to hold on to. You take the heart. You have a kingdom to save."

"Please, Henry. Take it." This time she put it into his hands, despite his protests. "When you awaken, you'll be able to live your life the way you've always dreamed. You can travel to any kingdom you'd like and become a royal guard. With all the skills you've developed here, I'll wager you'll be one of the best."

Henry laughed but then shook his head, wiping at rogue tears breaking through. "Your kingdom needs you," he said, putting the Ruby Heart back into her hands.

They sat in silence for a moment, exhausted . . . overwhelmed.

"We can figure this out together." Snow White laid the Ruby Heart to the side so she could take his hands again. "What were your two futures? Maybe there's a hint to all of this in what we saw."

"In one we went to battle," he said, but he seemed flustered by that possible future and moved on quickly. "In the other, Tabitha and I—"

He froze, his brows lowered, while he seemingly thought through his words as if trying to understand them. "Both Tabitha and I went home. Together."

Snow White's excitement was palpable, her understanding immediate. "Were you both touching the Ruby Heart?"

Henry's jaw dropped, then slowly slipped into a wide

grin, and he grabbed her face in his hands. "Stardrop, you're a genius!" he cried, and she laughed with joy at his words. "In the vision only I held the heart, but Tabitha was holding my hand!"

"We can all link hands in a long chain! And then—"

"Everyone in Diamant can go home," Henry finished, sounding more excited than she had ever heard him before.

They both whooped and hollered with excitement, joy unbridled, despite the disappointed tree still looming over them. Perhaps taking possession of the Ruby Heart had lifted whatever had been overshadowing the place. Because morning was breaking now. Golden rays cast a radiance onto their surroundings, chasing away the darkness.

They had won.

The Queen must have sensed her defeat and been wallowing in it, because the way home seemed shorter than the way there had, barely a day of travel. Snow White felt light on her feet, far too overjoyed to be fatigued, and it seemed like no time at all before she and Henry saw the sign for town. They smiled at each other and ran.

It was invigorating, running toward freedom that way.

Freedom . . . because any minute they would be going home. Their *actual* homes, in the real world, with their friends and families.

Any minute, they would wake up.

"Gather everyone in the square!" Henry called to those standing close by, his uncharacteristic enthusiasm catching them off guard. "Tell them we brought back the Ruby Heart! Hurry!"

Some people seemed confused, as if not able to process everything he was saying to them. But most of them ran, yelling, just as Snow White and Henry had done. Snow White and Henry looked at each other.

"I can't believe we did it," Henry said for perhaps the hundredth time since they'd found the Ruby Heart.

"And I knew we could," said Snow White, giving her friend a playful shove in the arm.

"Of course you did."

Snow White and Henry watched as the town bustled with both confusion and excitement.

"After all this time, I can finally leave this living nightmare behind." Henry paused and looked away, playing with the pearls around his neck as he said, "It is bittersweet, though—the thought that we might not remember any of this when we wake up."

Snow White looked at him slyly. "Is that your way of saying you'll miss me?"

"Miss *you*? The princess who runs headfirst into the face of danger?" He could barely keep a straight face. "No, but I'll miss this diamond sword, that's for sure—" He started as Tabitha nearly toppled him over with the force of her charging hug.

"I knew you two could do it," she said, and pulled Snow White into the hug. But abruptly, she looked around. "Where's Mouse?"

Snow White and Henry gave each other uncertain looks.

"I think it's better if we explain that to everyone at once," said Henry.

"Did something happen to her?" Tabitha asked, suddenly worried.

Snow White's heart sank. It all had happened so fast she hadn't had time to truly process the Queen's deception. A part of her mourned the lost friendship she'd had, though she knew it hadn't been real.

"She's gone," Snow White said.

Tabitha's eyes widened.

"But she wasn't real, Tab," Henry assured her. "She was a trick, sent by the Queen. She had all of us fooled."

Tabitha gave her brother a concerned look. "It can't be," she murmured.

"I'm sorry, it is," Snow White said, reaching for Tabitha's hand.

Tabitha's expression shifted from horrified to resolved. "Thank you, Snow White. We needed you."

The spark of friendship burned like a flame in Snow White's heart. Perhaps Tabitha had adapted better to Diamant than Henry had, but she was just as ready to go home as everyone else.

They took the time to make sure every single person was present. Once everyone had gathered, Henry handed Snow White the Ruby Heart. Then he held his hand out to her, and she smiled and took it, allowing him to help her step up onto the well.

Snow White turned to the people who had gathered in the town square. There was a mixture of confusion, fear, hope, and excitement. She looked at the Ruby Heart in her hands as it twitched each time the chambers pumped. And when the people saw it, there was no denying that it was exactly the legendary Ruby Heart they'd been searching for all those years.

Snow White held it up for everyone to see. "Henry and I followed the magic map and have brought back the Ruby Heart—not without difficulty, but we did it. There were many obstacles, but one of them wasn't something we ran into along the way. It was something we'd brought with us. Some*one*."

She tucked the Ruby Heart close to her chest, and the little butterfly in its cocoon eased her nerves. "Mouse didn't come back with us, because she's not who she says she is. Well, *wasn't*. She was a piece of the Queen's subconscious, put here to encourage us to enjoy ourselves, to put doubt in our minds about whether there was a way to go home. She never wanted any one of us to find the Ruby Heart. That was her only purpose here. And for far too long, she succeeded."

Shocked and horrified gasps echoed through the crowd. After all, they had known Mouse for years. It was unthinkable.

"Despite everything working against us," Snow White went on, "Henry and I brought back the Ruby Heart. This is our way to freedom—back to the waking world and the lives we knew. It's *real*. And all we have to do is trust each other enough to take each other's hands. It *will* take us home if we wish it."

For a long, excruciating moment, there was a thick silence. But then cheers and shouts of excitement rang out through the town. They were loud enough that they made Snow White wince before she burst into overjoyed laughter. All around, people were hugging each other, rushing to hold hands.

Henry stepped up beside the well with a proud smile on his face. "Well done."

Tabitha yelled out, "You heard her! We have to hold hands. Every last person, don't leave anyone out. We're all going home."

Looking around, seeing everyone gather, Snow White was suddenly overcome with emotion. Happiness, but at the same time . . .

Snow White looked at Henry as he diligently watched everyone from their perch on the elevated well platform to make sure they were all taking hands. How could she stand to leave such an amazing friend? *You have amazing friends back home who need saving,* she thought. But still. Why couldn't she keep everyone in her life? If only she could wake up and remember it all as a dream, at the very least.

But since no one knew what to expect upon waking, she leapt at Henry, wrapping her arms around his neck. He laughed, stumbling back a step as he squeezed her right back.

"I don't suppose we'll ever see each other again?" she asked, looking up at him after she'd given him a good, long hug.

"What happened to that optimism of yours?" he asked with a soft smile.

"What a horrible thought, to forget such a friend as you," Snow White said.

"Perhaps I will remember, Stardrop," he said, grinning widely. "And one day I'll travel to the castle and apply for the position of royal guard."

"I would love that," she said, beaming. "You deserve it, and so much more."

"Thank you for everything, my friend," Henry whispered.

"*We* did this. Together," said Snow White. Finally, she took a breath and held him at arm's length, looking up at him with hope. "It doesn't matter if we don't remember any of this when we wake up. True friendship can overcome anything, and you will always be my true friend in my dreams."

"Count on it," he said. He released Snow White and took his sister's hand on one side and her hand on the other, squeezing them both gently.

Snow White took one last look at Henry and Tabitha, who had done so much for her, who had sheltered and protected her when no one else did. Who had gone on this perilous journey with her, even though they were strangers. She had come to know them and love them, despite their short time together. They were true friends she hoped her heart would always remember, even if her mind did not.

"If you don't hurry up and make a wish . . ." Henry said teasingly.

"Oh, are you ready now?" she joked right back.

"Don't you know I've been ready for literal *years*?" But Henry's teasing demeanor dissipated as they looked at each other, as they saw in each other's eyes matching determination, boundless hope, and the true love of friendship. Henry gave Snow White a genuine smile. "Take us home, Stardrop."

Snow White nodded, her heart singing. She held the

Ruby Heart up in the palm of her hand as it pulsed and shimmered in the sunshine. And then she closed her eyes and made a wish.

Once upon a time, there was a girl with big dreams who fell into a deep sleep . . . and awoke to change her world for the better.